BLOTTO,
TWINKS
and the
Ex-King's
Daughter

BLOTTO, TWINKS

and the
Ex-King's
Daughter

SIMON BRETT

ROBINSON

Constable & Robinson Ltd
3 The Lanchesters
162 Fulham Palace Road
London W6 9ER
www.constablerobinson.com

First published in Great Britain by
Constable & Robinson Ltd 2009

This edition published by Robinson,
an imprint of Constable & Robinson Ltd 2010

A copy of the British Library Cataloguing in Publication
Data is available from the British Library.

UK ISBN: 978-1-84901-379-6

Printed and bound in the EU

1 3 5 7 9 10 8 6 4 2

To Pete,

who always had a taste for the silly

1

Blotto Finds a Body

'It's frightfully awkward, Mater, but I'm afraid there's a dead body in the library.'

'Not now, Blotto. We have guests.' And, on waves of breeding, perfume and fine silk, the Dowager Duchess of Tawcester wafted away from her younger son to continue being the perfect hostess. Her eyes sparkled semaphore to Grimshaw, the butler, indicating which of her guests should have their drinks topped up and, more importantly, which should not.

An expression of confusion took up residence in the face of the Right Honourable Devereux Lyminster. This was not unusual. The impossibly handsome features of the Dowager Duchess of Tawcester's younger son frequently wore an expression of confusion. The fine brow beneath his blond thatch would furrow, and lines would crinkle around his cornflower-blue eyes. Young women had on occasion been known to interpret this look as a sign of sensitivity and deep thought. They were invariably wrong in their estimation. Blotto's thoughts rarely ran deep enough to dampen the soles of his handmade brogues.

He refused the proffered champagne from the butler's silver salver. Devereux Lyminster drank little. His nickname certainly did not derive from his drinking habits. Amongst people of his class it was thought bad form for

1

nicknames to have logical explanations; they were items to be scattered about with random largesse, like small donations to charity.

'Grimshaw,' he murmured, 'you haven't seen Twinks, have you?'

'No, milord,' the butler replied. 'I believe her ladyship is still changing after her strenuous afternoon of tennis.'

'Oh, rodents!' The confusion on Blotto's face made room for a little anxiety.

'Was there something you wished your sister to sort out for you, sir?' Long experience had taught Grimshaw that this would indeed be the case. Blotto always turned to Twinks when faced with one of life's minor challenges, like which tie to wear or whom to marry.

'Yes. Bit of bother in the library.'

'What kind of bother?'

'Dead body.'

'I will deal with it at once, milord.'

Grimshaw enlisted the help of Harvey, who was one of the housemaids at Tawcester Towers. (Tawcester, it should be emphasized at this point, despite being spelt 'Taw-ces-ter', is pronounced 'Taster'. Everyone knows that.) That Harvey was considerably above the age of most housemaids, and that she had remained in employment after certain ethical lapses which might have ended other careers, reflected the fact that she had an agreement with the butler. The precise nature of this 'agreement' was something that the family and staff at Tawcester Towers were far too polite to investigate.

Harvey wore the black dress and apron of her calling. On most women such costume is expected to obscure the details of femininity; on Harvey it accentuated them. This was partly because of the unusually short length of dress that she (or perhaps more accurately Grimshaw) favoured. She carried a feather duster, though not in the expectation that it might be of much use in dealing with a dead body.

But it did give her an air of purpose. Any passing house guest or member of the staff would assume her to be engaged on some more innocent domestic mission.

The important point was that, from long experience of needing to, Grimshaw knew that he could trust Harvey's discretion. And he knew that dead bodies could threaten considerable inconvenience to the smooth running of a country house weekend. Below stairs, Tawcester Towers had hardly yet recovered from the shock of discovering Lord Tawcester himself, seated in front of his study fire with a face the colour of the vintage port which proved to be his final indulgence. And his lordship's demise had happened a full five years before.

The library, as most people of culture know, is one of the great glories of Tawcester Towers. It had been added during the substantial renovations of the property conducted by the seventh Duke, who unlike his predecessors, Black Rupert and Rupert the Fiend, had reversed the trend of losing the family money at cards. Instead he had proved himself an astute financial manager, had restored the Tawcester fortunes, expanded the Towers and earned the ungenerous nickname of Rupert the Dull.

The library is on the ground floor at the back of the mansion. Tall windows look out over the gently undulating fields of Tawcestershire, most of which is owned by the family. On the other three walls mahogany bookshelves, filled with symmetrical volumes, rise from floor to ceiling. The books are uniformly bound in brown leather with gilt lettering, and uniformly unread. Reading does not feature highly amongst the pastimes of the British aristocracy. Though many calves undoubtedly gave up their lives to provide bindings for their books, the Tawcester family tended to prefer their recreational killing to be more immediate. For them the inability to see what they were shooting at always took away much of the fun.

The impression should not be given that the Tawcesters

3

did not value their library. It was one of their proudest boasts, and no weekend house guest was in Tawcester Towers for more than half an hour before being invited to marvel at its splendours. The books were acknowledged to form a unique collection, and over the years many minor academics had been employed on the task of compiling and updating the catalogue. The Dukes of Tawcester had always had great respect for books; just so long as nobody expected them to read any.

The library had witnessed many scenes of misbehaviour and depravity – particularly during the time of Rupert the Dull's profligate heir Rupert the Libertine – but this was its first dead body ... (if one discounts domestics ... and in Tawcester Towers domestics had always been discounted. So the fact that in the early 1820s an under-housemaid had been crushed in the library by the descent of an ill-balanced bust of Homer had never even been mentioned to the ducal family. Staff problems had always been the butler's responsibility.).

The dead body which confronted the current butler and Harvey that afternoon was not in that state of serene repose recommended by the ancients for the final act of life. Its passing from the corporeal to the incorporeal had been neither willing nor elegant. Fortunately it was the body of a man, for the paroxysms which had preceded death would have rendered unbecoming the costume of a lady. He wore white tie and tails, the uniform that identified him as one of the Dowager Duchess's house guests. Which, Grimshaw recognized, was extremely inconvenient. Here was no servant, whose body could be discreetly shuffled off to the local undertaker with no questions asked. This death was going to require investigation.

'Shall I tidy him up, Mr Grimshaw?' asked Harvey. To her the butler was always 'Mr Grimshaw', even in private moments when a less formal appellation might have been expected. She stood, feather duster poised, as though that implement might somehow prove useful in the disposal of a corpse.

Grimshaw shook his head. 'I fear not. Until proved otherwise, this library must be treated as a crime scene.'

'You mean the police will have to be called?'

'Yes. And, once they have failed to identify the murderer, there will no doubt turn out to be a private detective among the Dowager Duchess's house guests, who will continue the investigation. Either way, the household is liable to undergo a period of irritating disruption.'

Harvey's feather duster quivered instinctively in her hand. 'So shouldn't I even dust him, Mr Grimshaw?'

'I fear not. At such moments, even the most basic instincts of domestic hygiene must be curbed.'

'How do you think he died, Mr Grimshaw?'

The butler's eyes narrowed as they focused on the contorted corpse before him. The face was claret red, eyes bulging, mouth gaping, hands still clasping at the throat as though to remove a collar that had been bought in too small a size.

'I would imagine it was something he ingested.'

'Poison?'

'That might be the logical conclusion which a professional investigator might reach, but it is not our place to reach conclusions, Harvey, logical or otherwise.'

'No, Mr Grimshaw.' There was a tentative silence before she continued, 'But might it be our place to speculate who the dead man is – or was?'

The butler conceded that it might be. The face, now so hideously distorted, had once been that of a good-looking young man, though of a sallow complexion that suggested he had not grown up on a diet of roast beef and Yorkshire pudding. Across his stiff shirt-front was a purple sash, clasped in place by a starburst of jewelled insignia. The flamboyance of this suggested that the man had not been trained in sartorial reticence by an English public school.

'My surmise would be,' said Grimshaw, 'that he is – or was – part of the entourage of the ex-King of Mitteleuropia.'

5

'I am sure you are right, Mr Grimshaw,' Harvey agreed. 'Are you going to ring the police?'

'Yes. That is my next duty.'

'Not yet!' The voice tinkled through the library like a cut-glass chandelier caught in the gentlest of zephyrs. But it was not a feeble voice. It carried the upper class authority that can only be developed by exploiting serfs through many generations.

The voice belonged to Lady Honoria Lyminster, known to her brother Blotto and everyone else the right side of the green baize door as 'Twinks'.

Her beauty had frequently been remarked on by the swarms of young swains who had fallen in love with her. But since they were all of her own class, their descriptions had rarely been more articulate than 'a fine filly', 'a corker', 'a bit of a looker' or 'an absolute bobbydazzler'. To do proper justice to her charms would have required the skills of a poet, and sadly, in the social circles where she moved, Twinks was never likely meet one.

But in the unimaginable event of a poet ever being invited to Tawcester Towers, he might have commented on the deep azure of her bewitching eyes, a complexion of ivory overlaid with rose petals, and ash-blonde hair spun as fine as the filigree of a spider's web. He might have lauded the fragile voluptuousness of her perfect figure, and observed that she moved in a way that made butterflies look clumping.

Had, however, this conjectural poet ever expressed such views to Lady Honoria Lyminster, he would have received the dismissive response, 'What guff!' Twinks was not unaware of her beauty; she just didn't regard it as important. There were more interesting things in her life. And of these the most interesting was acting as an amateur detective.

So the appearance of a dead body in the library in the middle of a particularly dreary house party was to Twinks a bonus comparable to finding a pearl in the grittiest of oysters.

At her arrival Grimshaw and Harvey had dutifully drawn back, to allow her unimpeded access to the body.

'Oh, larks!' she said. 'A poisoning at Tawcester Towers! Larksissimo!' She lowered her elegant head to the victim's mouth and sniffed the evanescent aroma of almonds. 'Cyanide – or I'm very much mistaken.'

Even had he been unaware of Twinks's exhaustive knowledge of toxins, Grimshaw would still have known his place sufficiently to say, 'I'm sure you are right, milady. Is there anything you wish me to do?'

'No, you and Harvey go back to the guests. Keep topping them up with bubbly. I'll just have a snoopy-snuffle round here.'

'And, milady, would you wish me to alert the proper authorities?'

'No, Grimshaw, I'll do it. I will summon the estimable Chief Inspector Trumbull. I like to do these things honourably – level playing field and all that. I must allow the police to have a fair wallop at the investigation ... before I run circles round them and tell them who really committed the murder.'

'Very good, milady.'

'Oh, there you are.' It was Blotto, who had just appeared in the doorway of the library. He nodded to Grimshaw and Harvey as they melted imperceptibly past him, then moved forward to his sister. 'Rum do, Twinks me old muffin. Bit of a candle-snuffer, isn't it?'

'But very jolly. Jollissimo!' The blue eyes sparkled like the scales of a leaping salmon caught in a shaft of sunlight.

'Do you recognize the poor old pineapple?'

'One of ex-King Sigismund's factotums.'

'Got a moniker for him?'

Blotto knew his sister would have. Had only to be introduced to someone once, and the name would stick in her retentive brain like a limpet. Whereas the interior of Blotto's brain had more in common with a well-used toboggan run; everything slid away down the sides.

'Captain Schtoltz, he was called.'

'Oh yes, vaguely remember the name from when they all arrived. Odd to be in ordinary evening blacks, though. If he was a Captain, why wasn't he wearing his dress uniform?'

'That, Blotto, is exactly the question I was asking myself.'

'Oh, really?' He was rather cheered to hear that. Blotto had accepted from an early age that, when it came to brain-power, his younger sister was a huge ocean liner to his little rowing boat. So to have actually had the same idea as her gave him quite a lift.

'And I think I know the answer,' Twinks went on.

'Well, don't keep it to yourself. Uncage the ferrets, old thing.'

'The reason Captain Schtoltz was not in uniform was . . .'

'Yes?'

'Because he was a spy.'

'Crikey.'

'Now, Blotto, will you hurry and get my camera? Before the peelers arrive with their hobnail boots to tread in all the evidence, I want to make a very detailed examination of the crime scene . . .'

2

The Police Are Called

Chief Inspector Trumbull had not been at the front of the queue when the intellect was handed out. Indeed, he appeared not to have been in the same county. But that did not prevent him from rising through the ranks of his chosen profession. Indeed, in those days for anyone in that profession to have shown intelligence or originality would have been a positive disqualification. The role of the police was to do a lot of boring legwork and paperwork, to trail up investigatory cul-de-sacs, to be constantly baffled, and dutifully amazed when an amateur sleuth revealed the solution to a murder mystery.

These skills Chief Inspector Trumbull possessed in abundance. He also knew his place, particularly when the aristocracy was involved. It therefore seemed to him entirely appropriate that he should obey the Dowager Duchess's summons to the Blue Morning Room before investigating the body in the library.

Though a deeply stupid man, Trumbull was not without bravery. But he, like most of his gender, always quailed in front of the Dowager Duchess of Tawcester. She was con-structed on the lines of a transatlantic steamer and it was comparably difficult to make her change her course once she was under way.

'Now, Trumbull . . .' she said to the quaking Inspector. She always called him 'Trumbull'. She would address appropriate royal personages by their titles, friends of her own class by their nicknames, and everyone else by their surname. For the Dowager Duchess the difference between a Chief Inspector, doctor, solicitor, vicar or under-housemaid was imperceptible. 'The main thing about this situation is that it's incredibly inconvenient. I have guests for the weekend.'

'Yes, Your Grace,' Trumbull concurred. 'Most unfortunate.'

'So I'm relying on you to treat the whole affair with all the sensitivity of which you are capable.'

'Oh, I'll certainly do that, Your Grace.' This was an easy promise to make. The amount of sensitivity of which Chief Inspector Trumbull was capable corresponded pretty well with that of a rhinoceros who'd woken up with a hangover and then sat on a hornets' nest.

'There will have to be an enquiry, will there?' Her words took the form of something she had learnt about in Latin lessons at school but long forgotten: 'a question expecting the answer no'.

Sadly, Chief Inspector Trumbull was unable to oblige. 'I'm sorry, Your Grace. I'm afraid the Chief Constable will insist on an enquiry.'

'Oh,' the Dowager Duchess mused. Needless to say, she had known the Chief Constable from birth. 'Bertie Anstruther . . . Maybe I should have a word with him . . .?'

'I'm afraid, until I receive orders to the contrary, Your Grace, I will be compelled to investigate this murder.'

'How tiresome. Still, if you have to . . .'

'May I ask, Your Grace, whether the fact of the . . . incident is already known to your guests?'

'Good Lord, no! I hope not. That wouldn't be much of a recommendation for Tawcester Towers hospitality, would it? Blotto and Twinks know, obviously.'

'I'm sorry?'

'My son and daughter.'

'Ah.'

10

'And a couple of the domestics . . . butler and one of the housemaids. Apart from that, no one.'

'Except for one person,' the Chief Inspector announced weightily.

'What are you talking about?'

'The murderer, Your Grace. The individual who committed the atrocity.'

'Good Lord, are you suggesting it was done by somebody in the house?'

'Geographical considerations alone would make that a likely possibility.'

'Hm.' The concept that the murder had required not only a victim but also a perpetrator had not occurred before to the Dowager Duchess. It was a double inconvenience. Then she saw a glimmer of reassurance in the gloom. 'But the murderer is not likely to tell anyone what he has done, is he?'

'Extremely unlikely, Your Grace.'

'Oh well, that's all right then. No social embarrassment there. Now, Trumbull, my guests are at dinner. I must join them very quickly. I am their hostess, after all.' She looked up at the ormolu clock on the carved mantelpiece. 'They will be on their fish course by now. I'm relying on you to have the whole thing cleared up before the ladies withdraw.'

'The whole thing?'

'Yes, your investigation. I want that done – and I want the body off the premises before the gentlemen go off to the billiard room.'

'But, Your Grace, that's not much more than half an hour away.'

'A lot can be achieved in half an hour. The conception of most children takes a considerably shorter time.' A very much shorter time when it had had anything to do with her, the Dowager Duchess recollected with distaste.

'Your Grace, it will be necessary for the purposes of my investigation for me to speak to your guests.'

'Speak to my guests? I am sorry, Chief Inspector, but you are not the kind of person to whom they are used to speaking.'

'Maybe not, Your Grace, but –'

'They include ex-King Sigismund of Mitteleuropia. Is he the kind of person whom you and Mrs Trumbull meet in your customary social round?'

'No, we do not.'

'Then why should you suddenly expect all the rules of society to be broken for you to be introduced to him?'

'A murder has been committed, Your Grace.'

'We don't know that. A person has died – that's all we know. There are many unfortunate circumstances that can cause people to die.'

'Yes, but, Your Grace –'

'I require your investigation – and the removal of the body – to be completed within the next half-hour, before the ladies withdraw and the gentlemen retire to the billiard room and the smoking room. Are you telling me it can't be done, Trumbull?'

The proper answer dallied on the edge of the Chief Inspector's lips. Distantly, from the earliest moment of his training, he remembered being told the duties of a policeman. Nobody was above the law. Investigations must all be carried out with the same punctilious and even-handed attention to detail, regardless of the status of the people involved. A policeman had to be incorruptible, concerned only with solving every crime with which he was presented.

'Very well, Your Grace,' he said. 'Half an hour it is.'

There was a Sergeant with whom Chief Inspector Trumbull always worked, and the law of averages might have dictated that this person should be more intelligent than his superior. This, however, was not the case. Sergeant Knatchbull was, if such a concept is possible, even less well intellectually endowed.

12

Their examination of the scene of crime did not therefore yield many startling insights, though there was a striking unanimity in their views of the situation. The man lying on the library floor was undoubtedly dead. Neither policeman questioned that. And from the expression on his face, both agreed that he had not departed this life in a relaxed and voluntary manner.

But beyond that ... 'A case for the experts,' concluded Chief Inspector Trumbull, showing fitting self-knowledge by not including himself in that category. He shrugged, not over-confident even of the skills of the 'experts' when they did come to examine the body. He had been through the same manoeuvres so many times before on other cases. Now, as he approached retirement, an innate laziness in him wanted to shorten the process. Why couldn't the whole business be speeded up? Why did he have to go through all the tedious preliminaries of investigating the case himself? Why couldn't a polymathic amateur sleuth arrive straight away and solve the thing?

Their cursory scene-of-crime examination completed, Chief Inspector Trumbull and Sergeant Knatchbull, with the help of Grimshaw, smuggled the body out of Tawcester Towers wrapped in a Turkish carpet. They used the back-stairs, confident they would not be seen at that time of the evening. It was not until later that the bolder and more inebriated male guests might enter that area in search of acquiescent chambermaids.

By the time dinner had ended, and the gentlemen adjourned to the billiard and smoking rooms, the body of Captain Schtoltz was already in the dicky of Chief Inspector Trumbull's car, joggling its way to Tawsworthy police station.

Lady Honoria Lyminster was quite a girl. Not only did she sometimes smoke cigarettes, she also actually had one of those new-fangled electric kettles in her bedroom and often made hot drinks without the intervention of either a cook or housemaid. It was thanks to her kettle that she and Blotto were sipping cocoa that evening. Twinks looked at her brother appraisingly. 'Well, you certainly seem to have hit the bull's-eye with ex-Princess Ethelinde.'

'What? Who're you talking about?'

'Ex-Princess Ethelinde. You know, Blotto. There's only one ex-Princess Ethelinde staying here. And she's as pretty as a cream tea with extra dollops of cream. Come on, you must've noticed. Ex-King Sigismund's daughter.'

'Oh, her.'

'She was eyeing you all evening like a cat over a gold-fish bowl. She certainly thinks you're the crystallized ginger.'

'Don't be a Grade A poodle, Twinks. Why would a breathsapper of a girl like that be interested in a prize chump like me?'

'Because you're dashed attractive – and a good bloke with it.'

'Oh, biscuits,' said Blotto, embarrassment spreading redly upwards from his wing collar.

'You're never going to find a bride if you can't spot the ones who're interested in you.'

'Well, I'm not sure that that matters so frightfully much. There are lots of things a chap can do in life without finding brides. Cricket and hunting and ... well ... adventures. In fact, from what I see, a lot of fellows would be much better off without brides. I mean, some of the boddos I used to be at school with have actually married Americans.'

Twinks let out a tinkling laugh. 'Well, at least nobody in our family has ever been reduced to that.'

'No, but in many ways I'm not sure that Loofah's done much better.'

Twinks couldn't argue about that. Their elder brother had drawn a bit of a short straw in the matrimonial stakes. (Not that the straw he had drawn was actually short. Sloggo, the new Duchess, towered over her chubby husband, and had limbs of such length that people suspected they had to be wound round something overnight, like a garden hose.) But Loofah – or to give him his proper name, Rupert Lyminster, Duke of Tawcester – had had no choice. The ducal line had to be continued and, much though he would have preferred to do it by some different method – *any* different method – there was no way of producing heirs that didn't involve marriage.

Of course Loofah hadn't had much of a say in his choice of bride. His mother had taken that on, as she did so many tasks at Tawcester Towers. And the Dowager Duchess knew that the purity of her daughter-in-law's breeding was much more important than such trifles as a pleasant personality or physical attractiveness. So she had selected Sloggo – known to readers of Debrett's as Lady Winifred Coules-Quick, eldest daughter of the Duke of Pargetshire – and a high society wedding was decreed.

The reports of that event in the Court Circular were appropriately decorous. Nowhere in their descriptions of the bride were the words 'maypole', 'clothesprop' or 'stick insect' used. Neither did anyone mention the Duke's nickname – not so exotic as 'Black Rupert' or 'Rupert the Fiend', but at least accurate – of 'Rupert the Fat'. Nor were the couple referred to in the press – as they had been by their less generous friends – as 'the bat and ball'.

Their union had proved to be efficient, in that it had so far produced two children. Both girls, though. This was a source of considerable aggravation to Loofah, because the continuing lack of a male heir meant he had to do it all over again.

'Anyway, Blotto me old gumdrop, don't let's talk about brides. Mummy'll sort one of those out for you when she thinks the time is right. Let's talk about something more interesting.'

'Anything's more interesting than marriage.'

'Yes, and this is really interesting. Another "M". Not "marriage", but "murder".'

Her brother looked blank for a moment, before recollection came to him. 'You mean the foreign pineapple in the library?'

'I certainly do.'

'Well, old Trumbull's come and had a shufti at him, so I suppose things are proceeding in their own sweet way.'

'What absolute guff! You know Trumbull's useless. He needs help to lick the butter off a crumpet. There's not a dabchick's chance in a foxhole that he's going to solve this crime. No, as usual, you and I are going to have to do it, Blotto.'

'Oh. But where do we start? The body's not even on the premises any more.'

'I know. But before Trumbull and his boneheaded assistant arrived, remember you got me my camera . . .?'

'Oh yes, so I did.'

'And I undertook a very quick but thorough examination of the scene of crime.'

Blotto was impressed. If his sister had focused the beam of her massive intellect on it, then the case was as good as solved. 'So who did it, Twinks?'

'I'm not quite there yet, old trouser button. But I did pick up a couple of pointers.'

'Like what?'

'Well, for a start, the late lamented wasn't murdered in the library.'

'Ah, you mean it was suicide . . . or some sort of ghastly accident gone wrong?'

'No,' Twinks replied patiently. 'I mean that he wasn't murdered *in the library*.'

Clouds gathered on Blotto's brow. Then miraculously they cleared. Sunshine broke through in a large beam. 'You mean he was stubbed out somewhere else and then his mortals were *moved into* the library?'

'Exactly that.'

'But how do you know?'

'Simple. I'd show you on a photograph, but it's still developing in that walk-in wardrobe I use as a darkroom.

But what it shows is that Captain Schtoltz's dinner jacket had been pulled up high around his neck, suggesting someone had lifted him under the armpits. Then, though there was still some warmth in the body, there was none on the area of library carpet on which it lay, which would imply he had been moved into that position quite recently. There were also scuff-marks on the carpet where his heels had dragged on the floor. Having taken a measurement of his shoes and estimated his body weight, I'm pretty sure from the angle of those indentations that Captain Schtoltz was placed in position by someone of well over average height.'

'Crikey, Twinks. I can never work out how all that brain fits into your dainty little cranium.'

She shrugged. 'Just a matter of logic. Keep your eyes wide open, Blotto, and eventually you'll see the relevant information.'

He sighed. He knew he could keep his eyes open as wide as they went and still not see the relevant information until it bit him on the leg. 'So what do we do – look for the tallest man in the ex-King's entourage and get Trumbull to arrest him?'

'It may not be quite that simple, Blotto. But looking for a tall man could be a good starting-point.'

'Righty-ho then.' Blotto was silent for a moment, then a modest gleam of energy flickered in his eye.

Twinks recognized the symptoms. Her brother had just had an idea. 'What is it?'

'I was just thinking . . .' he began slowly.

'Yes?'

'Most of the house guests will be asleep by now . . .'

'Undoubtedly.'

'. . . so it might be the perfect time to find our tall man.'

'Sorry. Not with you, Blotto?'

'Well, while they're asleep, they won't notice me creeping into their bedrooms . . .' He glowed with enthusiasm, as he always did when spelling out one of his ideas. 'And then when I'm in the bedrooms . . . I can look out and see which ones' feet stick out over the end of the bed . . .'

'Ye-es.'

'. . . so we'll know which ones are tall.'

Her brother looked so pleased at having reached this logical conclusion that Twinks didn't want to puncture his confidence. 'Good idea,' she said, and he glowed like a four-bar electric fire. 'But,' she continued gently, 'don't you think it might be simpler to wait till tomorrow morning, when all the house guests will be standing up?'

'What would be the advantage of that?' asked Blotto, confused.

'Well, when they're standing up, we'll be able to see which ones are tall.'

He didn't enjoy having his good idea rejected. 'That would be another way of doing it,' he conceded. 'Why, what are they all going to be doing tomorrow?'

'Hunting.'

'Ah.' The customary smile was reinstated on Blotto's handsome features. Now they were talking about something he understood.

3

A-Hunting We Will Go!

It was one of those autumn days that made one feel even sorrier for people who hadn't had the good luck to be born in England. The low morning sun peeked through the trees of the Tawcester Towers estate like a debutante at her first ball waiting to be asked to dance. The leaves on the ancestral oaks flashed russet and gold. Gleefully beyond the ha-ha hares scampered, their white scuts held arrogantly high. Pheasants too strutted across the grounds, imperious in their immunity. Nothing which was about to happen was their problem. Today the foxes were going to get it.

Blotto breathed in the crisp air of his native country and his lungs expanded with satisfaction. His black hunter Mephistopheles felt firm between his thighs, and little tremors of excitement communicated themselves between horse and man. Blotto listened to the distant burble of the countryside and the closer sounds of hooves stamping, hounds baying and members of his own class honking. His eyes took in the red of the huntsmen's coats, the contrasting black of Grimshaw and his staff serving the stirrup cups, and his heart swelled with pride. This was England at its most glorious. This was a scene that would last for ever. There would never be anyone so unpatriotic or humourless – or common – as to put an end to hunting.

He looked over to the main steps that led up to the columned portico of Tawcester Towers. His mother stood there, unwillingly relying on the support of a stick. During the previous hunting season her horse Caligula had refused at a particularly high fence and catapulted his aristocratic cargo over it. The resulting broken hip had not yet fully mended, and the Dowager Duchess's quack had had the temerity to say she was not yet ready to ride to hounds again. Her instinct had been to ignore the common little man's advice, and only the combined and forceful arguments of Loofah, Twinks and Blotto had dissuaded her. But she was determined to knit her fractured bones back together as soon as possible by sheer willpower. It wouldn't be long before she'd be back in the saddle. There were still foxes out there that had her name on them.

She looked with undisguised contempt at the woman standing beside her. Ex-King Sigismund's ex-Queen Klara had no physical excuse for not getting up on a horse. She just didn't enjoy hunting. Worse, she had been heard to declare that she thought it unladylike.

The Dowager Duchess had no time for such pusillanimity. Through narrowed eyes she contemplated her unwanted companion for the day. Ex-Queen Klara was not a thing of beauty. Her daughter's good looks clearly came from ex-King Sigismund's side of the family, and indeed ex-Princess Ethelinde's conception must have required a considerable effort of will on his part. Nor was the fact that the ex-Princess had no siblings much of a surprise. Ex-Queen Klara was no doubt an admirable woman in many ways, but certainly not in the way that might make men fall in love with her. She didn't have come-to-bed eyes; they were at best let-me-tuck-you-up eyes. And in her construction, the Almighty had not stinted on materials. Indeed, in the event of anarchists throwing bombs, there was no woman one would rather have between oneself and the explosion. Which, given the volatile state of Mitteleuropian politics, was maybe, from her husband's point of view, a large part of ex-Queen Klara's attraction.

The Dowager Duchess ceased her scrutiny of her guest, having decided that she'd just have to make the best of it.

Her education had not only reinforced the Dowager Duchess's sense of her own rightness at all times, it had also taught her to find the positives in any situation. No way round it, she couldn't go hunting. But she could still pass the day amiably enough in another of her favourite pursuits, patronizing a foreigner.

Blotto took the proffered silver stirrup cup from the outstretched tray and realized that he didn't recognize the footman who was outstretching to proffer it. 'New, are you?'

'Yes, milord.' He had the fastidious look of a man who had just opened the box of a three-week-old Camembert. Blotto liked that in a footman.

'Do you have a name?' Most of them seemed to, after all.

'Pottinger, milord.'

The man's vowels were very uncouth. Must be odd, thought Blotto in a rare moment of reflection, to grow up making noises like that. Bit like being foreign. Made sense, though, with the servant classes. Left them in no doubt of their inferiority. Every time they opened their mouths, they knew they'd missed out in the breeding stakes. So did everyone who heard them. Same with foreigners too, when you came to think of it. No, by and large, the world was pretty well organized.

'Pottinger, eh? Well, I hope you'll enjoy yourself here at Tawcester Towers.'

'I have no doubt at all that I shall, milord.'

Feeling that he had demonstrated enough common touch for one day – or indeed for the rest of the year – Blotto turned away from the footman and raised the stirrup cup to his mother. She waved gracious acknowledgement and he took a long swallow. Superb. Grimshaw's recipe ignored conventional wisdom and put in three times as much real brandy as the insipid cherry variety. The result was a drink whose impact ought to have left a neat exit wound at the back of the imbiber's head.

Energized, Blotto contemplated the blissful day which lay before him. Endless hours of crashing over the local farmers' fields and through their fences, with at the end the uncomplicated pleasure of seeing a fox torn apart by the hounds. Nothing else to think about. What more could a chap want?

Then he caught his sister's eye and remembered that he had got something else to think about. Twinks looked magnificent in her black hunting costume, side-saddle on her fine white mount Persephone. She too appeared all set for some carefree hours of carnage. But the look that the perfect blue eyes flashed through the veil at her brother reminded him that their day had another purpose. They were assessing the house guests to find one who fitted the role of murderer.

Now Blotto knew that one way of identifying a murderer was by assessing the motive they might have had for committing the crime, or by recognizing the kind of personality that might behave in such an ungentlemanly manner. But he left that kind of deep intellectual stuff to Twinks. The only clue he'd got, from her, was that the chap they were looking for was tall. So he looked around the meet for someone tall.

Looking at people on horseback is not the best way of assessing their height, because it can be a bit tricky to know which bit is man and which bit is horse. But Blotto knew every animal in the Tawcester Towers stables and how many hands high each one of them was, to the last fraction of a fingernail. (When it came to hunting or cricket his knowledge was encyclopedic; at school it had been the more traditionally academic subjects that let him down.) So, in the moments before the horn sounded for the start of the hunt, he mentally measured every one of the Mitteleuropian entourage. It didn't occur to him to assess the height of any of the more local house guests. To Blotto's rather straightforward mind, it was impossible that anyone British could have done something so ghastly as commit murder.

He didn't have to look far. On horses either side of ex-King Sigismund sat two very tall blond men in black riding habits. They appeared to be identical and, but for the cruel set of their thin lips, might have been good-looking. The way the men's slate-grey eyes darted back and forth beneath colourless lashes suggested they fulfilled some kind of bodyguard function to the ex-King.

Well, that was pretty damned easy, thought Blotto. Must remember when the day's hunting's finished to get Chief Inspector Trumbull to arrest one of those chappies. Or both, just to be on the safe side.

But then the hunting horn sounded. Mephistopheles and Blotto stepped forward, horse and man fused into one quivering mass of muscle and excitement.

Having identified his quarry – that is his human quarry rather than the fox – Blotto had intended during the hunt to keep the ex-King's bodyguards under pretty close surveillance. But, as ever, the rush of excitement engendered by the mere thought of a fox swept all other thoughts from his head. And then, when the stream of hounds and horses had only smashed down half a dozen farmers' fences, he was distracted by a more pressing priority.

Ex-King Sigismund's daughter, the ex-Princess Ethelinde, had been very prettily mounted on a small horse – only just too big to be a pony – called Boxer. Twinks had ridden him for years, and under her he'd been as docile as a bribed local councillor. But sensing a less dominant personality in his saddle, Boxer had quickly recognized the opportunity to misbehave. Lulling the ex-Princess into a false sense of security by taking the first few hedges with exemplary poise at the back of the cavalcade, the horse found his break when they reached a larger field bordering a small wood. Gleefully diverting from the main body of the hunt, he set off at breakneck speed for the shelter of the trees.

Ex-Princess Ethelinde, whose previous riding experience had been on biddable Mitteleuropian trotting mares, had no skills to deal with this new development. The possibility of her having any control over Boxer was a fantasy. It was all she could do to cling on to the pommel of her side-saddle as she was tossed back and forth on the horse's back like a rag doll.

Seeing her predicament, Blotto did not hesitate. With a tug on the reins and a squeeze of his thighs, he changed his giant hunter's course and sent him speeding after the hapless ex-Princess. Mephistopheles thundered over the field towards his quarry.

They made it just in time. Boxer knew full well that the low branches of the trees would quickly sweep any irritant rider off his back, which was exactly why he had gone straight for them. And a bough as solid as a metal bar was only inches away from ex-Princess Ethelinde's pretty face when Boxer's reins were snatched and he was pulled off course by the galloping Blotto.

The truculent beast was turned to face away from the woods and subdued by a sharp word of reproof. Boxer looked balefully up at Blotto, but knew better than to argue with his authority. The colour came and went from ex-Princess Ethelinde's cheeks as she struggled to regain her breath and composure.

It was the first time Blotto had really looked at her. As a rule, having been to English public school, he felt awkward in the presence of women outside his immediate family. But, spurred on in some measure by what Twinks had said about the ex-Princess's interest in him, he did a quick survey of the goods on offer.

In spite of her distressed state, ex-Princess Ethelinde was clearly quite a looker. The hair that peeped from under her riding hat might have looked black, but contrasted with the jetty fabric of her dress, it showed lights of glowing chestnut. Eyes the colour of coffee beans were set in a pale face of exquisitely proportioned features. The lips through which her anxious breaths came and went were as red and luscious as loganberries. The whole package had been assembled with exemplary neatness and skill.

'Um . . .' said Blotto. He had found that was a pretty safe opening gambit with women.

'I cannot thank you enough.' The ex-Princess's voice was huskily accented. Must be odd, thought Blotto, growing up somewhere like Mitteleuropia, wasting all that time mastering a foreign language. To get ahead in life, you're going to have to learn English eventually. Be much simpler and more logical if everyone spoke it from birth.

'Well . . . you know,' he said modestly.

'I knew you were a fine gentleman, but I did not know you were also a hero.'

'Oh, biscuits,' said Blotto. He didn't like this rather effete Continental habit of praising chaps. Surely the British way was better? Someone does something good, and nobody mentions it. Saves a lot of embarrassment all round.

'I would not wish,' the ex-Princess continued, 'for it to have happened because of my having been in danger, but I am pleased that you and I have a chance to be alone together. During the rest of my stay here there have always been many people about us.'

'Yes, true.' But Blotto wasn't convinced by her argument. At school he'd always been surrounded by other chaps. 'Mind you, I always think it's nice to have a crowd around. Don't you?'

'Not when you want to be alone with someone, no.'

Her voice was so soft and breathy that Blotto became rather concerned. 'I say, have you got a touch of the old asthmatics? Or something gone down the wrong way? Would it help if I gave you a bit of a thump on the back?'

'It might help,' the ex-Princess said coyly, 'if you were to hold my hand . . .'

'Oh, I don't think holding hands is much good for choking fits, you know,' said Blotto.

Ethelinde tried again. 'I have never been so happy as being here at Tawcester.' She gave full weight to each of the place name's syllables.

'No, sorry,' said Blotto, 'it's pronounced "Taster".'

'Why?'

He'd never in his life been asked such a peculiar question. 'Well, because it is,' he replied. 'Anyway, glad you're having a bit of a lark here at the Towers. Lovely part of the world, isn't it? Best part of the entire world, actually. I mean, I haven't actually been everywhere else in the world, but some things you just know instinctively, don't you? I'm sure there's nowhere in any foreign country that's as beezer to look at as Tawcestershire.'

'The world is full of many beautiful things, Devereux.' Again she accentuated each syllable and made the last one sound like 'ooks'.

'Actually, it's not said like that.'

'So how is it said?'

Pronunciation clearly wasn't her strong suit, and he didn't want to draw attention to the deficiency. So he just said, 'Everyone calls me Blotto.'

'Why?'

No question about it, poor girl wasn't really very bright. 'Because they do,' he replied. 'Tell me one thing,' he continued, because he had been taught that a good conversationalist asks about the people he's conversing with, 'what does it feel like being foreign?'

'I do not understand your question. In Mitteleuropia I am not regarded as "foreign".'

'Maybe not, but you know you are really. I just wondered how it felt . . . ?'

'If you came to Mitteleuropia . . . Blotto . . .' she pronounced the nickname with care, 'you are the one who would be "foreign".'

He roared with laughter. Girl might not be very bright, but she certainly had a sense of humour.

'I hope one day,' she said softly, 'you will come and see me in Mitteleuropia.'

Blotto couldn't think of any reason why he'd ever want to do that. He'd heard the hunting wasn't bad out there, but it would have to be exceptionally good to get him to go to a foreign country. Still, his manners told him that probably wasn't the thing to say to her. So he replied, safely, 'Sounds hoopee-doopee.'

The dark brown eyes sparkled. 'You mean you would like to see more of me?'

It had worked the last time, so he fell back on another 'Sounds hoopee-doopee.'

He didn't quite know why she then seized his arm with such intensity. Probably still in a state of shock after her narrow escape from the horizontal branch.

'Oh, Blotto . . .' the ex-Princess cooed, 'you are such a man.'

'Oh, yes,' he agreed. 'Have been from birth.'

Then he realized that he was frittering away a good day's hunting. Having ascertained that ex-Princess Ethelinde was too shaken to continue the sport herself, he summoned a huntsman to escort her back to Tawcester Towers. Thus providing the Dowager Duchess with the bonus of another foreigner to patronize.

4

The ex-King's Troubles

The Dowager Duchess, taking a break from her patronizing duties, was on the way up to her dressing room before lunch, when she saw Harvey stretching with her feather duster to reach one of the mounted stags' heads in the Main Hall. The shortness of the housemaid's skirt and the extent of her stretch meant that she was showing far more leg and underwear than is usually thought appropriate in polite society. The view was being relished by the Tawcester Towers butler who was, not to put too fine a point on it, gawping.

'Grimshaw,' the Dowager Duchess's voice bellowed across the cavernous space, 'don't drool!'

'I am so sorry, Your Grace. I did not see you there.'

'Evidently. And, Harvey,' the Dowager Duchess bellowed, 'you will go immediately and change into some undergarments less redolent of an Egyptian cabaret!'

The housemaid dutifully yes-Your-Graced and scurried off towards the back staircase, as if about to make the requested sartorial modification. But she had no intention of changing a thing. When it came to a conflict between the demands of Tawcester Towers' Dowager Duchess and its butler, Harvey knew where her loyalties lay. She wasn't about to deprive Mr Grimshaw of anything he liked.

The Dowager Duchess summoned the butler to her with

an imperious flick of her finger. 'Remind me,' she said. 'What is the situation between you and Harvey?'

He smiled suavely. 'We are teetering on the brink of matrimony, Your Grace.'

'It seems to me, Grimshaw, you've been teetering rather a long time. Seventeen years is, by anyone's reckoning, a pretty long teeter.'

'One wants to be sure, Your Grace.'

'If you're not sure by now, you're a less solid character than I'd always had you down for. Do something about your marital status, Grimshaw.'

'Yes, Your Grace.'

'Make an honest woman of Miss Harvey.'

'It is too late, I fear, for that to be achieved, Your Grace.'

'Yes, I suppose it is. Well, marry her, anyway.'

'I will put the matter in train, Your Grace.'

The butler smiled, bowed and retreated towards his pantry, with no intention of making any change in his domestic circumstances. He and Harvey had an understanding. No amount of badgering from the Dowager Duchess would be allowed to change the status quo. And he felt pretty sure that his employer was well aware of that situation.

The Dowager Duchess, who *was* well aware of that situation, snorted and continued up the stairs.

Then the butler remembered that he did have something of importance to pass on to his employer. 'Your Grace . . .'

She stopped in mid-stride. 'Yes?'

'There was a telephone communication this morning from Chief Inspector Trumbull.'

'Oh, to let us know that everything was sorted out with that unpleasant business in the library?'

'No, Your Grace. Chief Inspector Trumbull was very apologetic, but he said that he did need to speak to some of your house guests about the incident.'

'What nonsense,' said the Dowager Duchess pettishly. 'I can't have my house guests disturbed over something trivial like that. I'll have to have a word with the Chief Constable about that disruptive little man.'

'It was at the Chief Constable's insistence that Chief Inspector Trumbull made his request, Your Grace.'

'Was it? Then I will certainly have to have a word with him.'

The Dowager Duchess changed direction and stomped back down to the hall and Tawcester Towers' one telephone. She got through to the Chief Constable and gave him a good ear-bending. She reminded Bertie that she had known him when he was in short petticoats in the nursery. She reminded him that he had been at the same school as the late Duke and the current Duke. And she reminded him that, even though – because of certain indiscretions by his mother – Bertie Anstruther was not quite the genuine article, he had still been invited to Tawcester Towers on more than one occasion. She emphasized the code of behaviour which exists between people of a certain class and ordered him to rescind the order he had given to Chief Inspector Trumbull.

The Chief Constable refused. The Dowager Duchess was reduced to a state of fury. And when she was reduced to a state of fury, someone had to suffer for it. Ex-Queen Klara and ex-Princess Ethelinde were in for a pretty humiliating lunch.

Lunch on the hunting field was not something of which Blotto approved. On days when he was out on Mephistopheles, he relished a good wallop at the chafing dishes round breakfast time and then, after some seven or eight hours in the saddle, a real belt-buster of a dinner.

But of course on that particular day they'd got Continentals with them, and when it came to their stomachs Continentals were always rather effete. So a halt in the proceedings was called at a hunting lodge on the outskirts of the Tawcester Towers estate. Grooms appeared to arrange temporary accommodation for the horses. It all seemed a ridiculous upheaval to Blotto, who reckoned the only possible beneficiary of the interruption was the fox. Still, a large alfresco picnic had been organized, and Blotto was too well brought up not to take advantage of the proffered break.

He would have expected Twinks to have been equally irritated by the disruption of the day's hunting, but she seemed almost to welcome the delay. 'Be a chance to talk to the ex-King's people in a relaxed way,' she hissed at her brother as he passed. 'Maybe pick up some clues.'

'Oh yes, right, tickey-tockey,' said Blotto, who had completely forgotten about the investigative intentions of the day. When he was hunting he had great difficulty in bringing his mind to bear on anything else. In fact, when he wasn't hunting, he had great difficulty in bringing his mind to bear on anything else. Except cricket, of course.

'So socialize, Blotto. Ask pertinent questions.'

'Right you are, old thing.' There was a long silence. 'Um . . . what sort of questions might be pertinent?'

'Anything to do with Captain Schtoltz.'

'Oh. Yes. Of course.'

It was a beautiful scene. An ex-King with his exiled courtiers in a clearing of a forest whose leaves were turning slowly crisp and gold. Some people might have been aware of an *As You Like It* parallel, the ex-King like the banished Duke in the Forest of Arden. Such a comparison would have been lost on Blotto. He'd never quite hit it off with Shakespeare. Or any other poet. Any writer, come to that. He had always been quite content for Twinks to take on the role of family brainbox.

The Tawcester Towers staff, making no concession to the outdoor setting, had set up long tables and chairs for the hunters. Silver tableware shone on top of stiff white linen. The food was excellent too. Joints of beef, hams, haunches of venison. Game pies. Perfect wines, of course. Champagne chilled with ice from the ice house, robust, chubby clarets.

31

The scene made ex-King Sigismund maudlin and nostalgic. And in his maudlin nostalgia, he indulged in that rather regrettable habit so characteristic of displaced Continental monarchs – boasting.

'Of course in Mitteleuropia we have hunting parties much bigger than this. Around my Castle of Berkenziepenkatzen, which is only fifty miles from our capital, Zling, there I have the best hunting in the entire world.'

Blotto found this kind of talk, as well as being embarrassing, slightly pathetic. He was the last chap in the world to show off or score points, but the fact that the world's best hunting was to be found in Tawcestershire was self-evident to the meanest intellect. Well, Blotto knew his own intellect to be pretty mean, and it was self-evident to him. To suggest that the hunting round the Castle of Berkenziepenkatzen – wherever that might be – could match the facilities round Tawcester Towers was the gibbering of an idiot.

Blotto was also again struck – as he had been in the presence of ex-Princess Ethelinde – by the inconvenience of not having English as one's first language. The ex-King's accent was deep and thick and there were a lot of perfectly simple words he just couldn't pronounce properly.

Also, Blotto thought, the chap might have had a bad deal from life, but he did rather wallow in it. Losing a kingdom might be a candle-snuffer on the perkiest of spirits, but there still came a time when you just had to stop crying over spilt milk and put the lid on it . . . or mop it up . . . or . . . Blotto wasn't very good at metaphors.

'When I return in triumph to my rightful kingdom,' Sigismund continued with mournful relish, 'I will invite all your family –' he nodded to Twinks and Blotto – 'to enjoy the hospitality of Berkenziepenkatzenschloss.'

'That's very kind,' said Twinks politely. 'It would be such a lark.'

Blotto agreed effusively, though the thought running through his mind went: Come off it, I'm as likely to go there as I am to clean my own shoes.

Then, feeling that perhaps he ought to contribute more to the conversation, he asked, 'And when is that likely to be?'

'When is what likely to be?'

'When you return in triumph to your rightful kingdom?'

It seemed not to have been the right question. There was an uneasy rumbling amongst his retinue and the ex-King's brows, already dark, darkened a few more shades.

'I will return to my rightful kingdom when the vile usurper of my throne is overthrown!'

'Ah,' said Blotto. 'Right. Sorry, not terribly up with Mitteleuropian politics. So who is this vile usurper chappie?'

Again the retinue was uneasy. Some glanced at the ex-King nervously, as if expecting an eruption of anger. But the exiled monarch seemed prepared graciously to dissipate the fogs of Blotto's ignorance.

'The man who has stolen the throne of Mitteleuropia is none other than my own brother, Vlatislav. The man I trusted like my own brother . . .'

'But I thought you said he was your own brother?'

'Of course. That is why I trusted him like my own brother.'

'Ah. Right,' said Blotto.

'Vlatislav was my Minster for War.'

'Do you have a lot of war in Mitteleuropia?'

'Everywhere in Europe there is always war. A war that has just ended, a war that is just about to start, a war that has been bubbling under like lava in a volcano for many years.'

'Right. So how did this Vlatislav johnnie actually seize the throne?'

The ex-King sighed and his retinue sighed with him. This tale of perfidy had been told many times, and grown in the telling. Now it had become almost a religious ritual. Ex-King Sigismund began: 'Four years ago I leave Mitteleuropia with my family at the invitation of my second cousin, King Anatol of Transcarpathia. We are to spend a month at his summer residence by the lake at Bad Vibesz. Little did I know that for some years my brother had been making plans behind my back to usurp my rightful throne. He had suborned the military, promised to divide up the bulk of my estates among the aristocracy, bribed the middle classes with promises of tax-cuts, and the lower classes with free beer. Two days after our arrival in Bad Vibesz I discover he has organized a coup.'

Feeling some response was required, Blotto said, 'Coo.'

'Yes, coup,' said ex-King Sigismund.

'No, I just meant "Coo".'

'"Coup"?'

'Oh, never mind,' said Blotto.

'But couldn't you, Your Majesty,' asked Twinks, 'have mounted a counter-coup with the help of King Anatol of Transcarpathia?'

'Tuh,' said ex-King Sigismund dismissively. 'King Anatol is a nothing. He talks a good war, but when it comes to reality, he is a craven coward.'

'Oh dear.'

'The same is true of his son, Crown Prince Fritz-Ludwig. He is full of promises. He says he will recapture my kingdom for the love of the Princess Ethelinde, but when it comes to what you call the munch –'

'"Crunch", I think,' said Twinks tactfully.

'Yes, when it comes to the "crunch" . . . like his father, Crown Prince Fritz-Ludwig is also a broken reed.'

The good thing about this exchange, from Blotto's point of view, was the news that ex-Princess Ethelinde had another admirer. If Crown Prince Fritz-Ludwig of Transcarpathia, despite being a broken reed, continued to do what was expected of him, then maybe she'd shift her romantic aspirations away from the denizens of Tawcester Towers. Blotto knew lots of women who'd married broken reeds, and it didn't seem to have done them much harm.

'No, for many years Vlatislav had been planning his evil coup . . .'

Blotto decided not to interject another 'Coo' into this pause. It might be wise to avoid complication.

'Even when we were infants in the nursery, Vlatislav always envied what belonged to me. I remember, when I was a mere four years old, he . . .'

While this litany of fraternal betrayal continued and Blotto's eyes began to glaze over, those of his sister, bright and observant, flickered round the assembled luncheon-eaters. The ex-King's entourage comprised some dozen gentlemen. (Their servants were, needless to say, not involved in the hunting. They stayed below stairs at Tawcester Towers, being patronized by the resident staff. Twinks made a mental note to ask Grimshaw to question them about Captain Schtoltz.) In hunting dress the Mitteleuropians looked only slightly less ridiculous than they did the rest of the time. The ex-King and his acolytes had very Continental tastes in the matter of uniforms. The concept that one could have too much gold leaf or frogging, that there might be a desirable limit to the number of tassels, chains or medals attached to a jacket, seemed not to have occurred to them. Twinks had seen department store Christmas trees with less decoration.

The men around the ex-King were mostly, like him, shortish and of dark complexion, so the two tall blond bodyguards made a striking contrast. At the beginning of the luncheon, Twinks had contrived to have herself introduced to them. Their names were Zoltan and Bogdan, and their mutual surname Grittelhoff suggested that they were at least brothers. A closer look at them confirmed that they were identical twins. Neither partook of any wine at the meal, and the constant vigilance of their grey eyes suggested that, even here under the protection of Tawcester Towers, they feared for the safety of their royal charge.

Their courtesy on meeting Twinks had been exemplary, and each had assured her how much he was enjoying his stay in the 'beautiful English sidecountry', but the words they spoke were automatic. The smiles on their thin lips brought no echoing glow to their eyes. And the way they handled their cutlery at the luncheon suggested that both brothers had experience in using knives for more sinister purposes.

One thing that had struck Twinks was how little the disappearance of Captain Schtoltz from their midst seemed to have affected the ex-royal party. So, boldly, in her conversation with Zoltan and Bogdan Grittelhoff she asked after the whereabouts of the man to whom she had been introduced on his arrival, but whom she had not seen since.

'Ah, Captain Schtoltz has had to leave the party,' Zoltan Grittelhoff replied.

'Indeed,' Bogdan Grittelhoff agreed. 'For him it was necessary to go off on a special mission away from England.'

Well, he didn't get far. He didn't even leave Tawcester Towers. But Twinks kept such thoughts to herself. 'Who was the special mission for?' she asked.

'For the King,' replied Zoltan Grittelhoff.

'Oh, surely you mean "the ex-King"?'

As soon as the words were out of her mouth, she knew they were the wrong ones. The brothers stood up straight, clasped their right arms across their breasts, and Bogdan Grittelhoff spoke for both of them when he said, 'There is only one King of Mitteleuropia. That is King Sigismund. Soon the traitor Vlatislav will be defeated and the crown will be returned to its rightful owner – King Sigismund!'

Like the ex-King's own recounting of his woes, this statement carried overtones of a religious incantation.

At that point both brothers bowed and moved away, muttering to each other in their own guttural tongue. Twinks was left with the distinct feeling that, in an important matter of Mitteleuropian royal etiquette, she had been found wanting. Honestly, these Continentals were so sensitive. They set such store by the piffling difference between a 'King' and an 'ex-King', almost as if their monarchy had the same kind of history and significance as the British one.

But Twinks barely had time to have the thought, because she caught the words the Grittelhoff brothers exchanged as they left her. Which put a completely new gloss on the situation. She couldn't wait to tell Blotto.

She had to wait until they were remounting after the meal, and she found her brother somewhat out of sorts. He hadn't approved of taking a luncheon break in the first place and now he felt too replete with food and wine to appreciate fully the thrill of the chase. On top of that, he had had to listen to an ex-regal monologue about what felt like two millennia of Mitteleuropian history.

'Captain Schtoltz was going on a special mission,' Twinks hissed at him. 'The ex-King doesn't even know the man's dead.'

'Are you sure?' asked Blotto, jolted out of his grumpiness.

'Yes,' Twinks replied. 'But though the ex-King doesn't know, his bodyguards certainly do.'

'Really?'

'Yes. Just as they were leaving me, I heard them say that they'd have to be careful, that I was getting too curious about Captain Schtoltz's death.'

'Good gracious,' said Blotto. 'You heard them say that?'

'Definitely.'

'Nice of them to talk in English, so that you could understand what they were saying.'

'No, Blotto, they talked in Mitteleuropian.'

'Did they? Gosh, Twinks, do you speak Mitteleuropian?'

'Enough to get by.'

'Crikey! Is there no end to your talents?'

She laughed with fitting girlish modesty. But actually the answer to his question was no. Twinks could basically do everything.

5

Revelations at the Dinner Table

The day's hunting concluded with the ritual dismantling of a fox by the hounds. Which was as it should have been. But the climax didn't bring Blotto the effusion of pure joy that he usually felt at such moments. Breaking for luncheon had thoroughly taken the gloss off the day for him. They should have done the hunting in the proper way, not kowtowed to their guests' predilection for gastronomic mollycoddling.

As he dressed for dinner that evening he still felt disgruntled. Normally he would have been in high spirits after a day in the field, and ravenous for the meal ahead. But the luncheon had taken the edge off his appetite. He wasn't in his customary state of being 'as hungry as a hunter'.

Add to that, he was having great difficulty pressing the stud through the slits of his wing collar. He would really have to speak to Grimshaw. Somebody in the laundry must have been slapping on the starch like it was going out of fashion. He knew he could ring for his manservant Tweedling to fix the collar for him, but he didn't want to. There were areas of his life where Blotto liked to show his independence.

A tap sounded on his dressing-room door. 'Come in, Twinks,' he said. Nobody else would have had the temerity or lack of breeding to enter his inner sanctum.

The visitor was indeed his sister, a shimmering vision in an evening dress and matching snood of mother-of-pearl silk.

'Hello, Twinks. You've arrived just in the nick of time. I'm about to garrotte myself with this spoffing useless contraption.'

'Let me . . .' In a matter of seconds her deft fingers had the recalcitrant collar anchored to its studs. 'Listen, Blotto . . .'

'Yes, me old biscuit barrel?'

'We mustn't lose vigilance.'

'No, no certainly not.' A confused silence. 'Vigilance about what?'

'The Grittelhoff brothers knew about Captain Schtoltz's disappearance. We must find out how many others of the Mitteleuropian party do as well.'

'Righty-ho.' Another confused silence. 'How do we do that?'

'We ask them. But subtly.'

'Tickey-tockey,' said Blotto, sounding more confident than he was. Self-knowledge wasn't his strong suit, but he did know that the words 'Blotto' and 'subtly' didn't often appear in the same sentence. 'May be simpler, old pineapple, if you just tell me exactly what you want me to do . . .'

'Very well. I want you to concentrate on ex-Princess Ethelinde.'

'Oh?'

'She already thought you were the cat's pyjamas before you rescued her in the hunting field this morning . . .'

'Oh, biscuits,' said Blotto.

'Now she thinks you're the retriever's nightie.'

Her brother shrugged. 'Didn't do anything any other chap wouldn't have done in the same gluepot.'

'Nevertheless, the ex-Princess can't refuse you anything. She only has eyes for you.'

'Don't talk such toffee, Twinks. Apparently, according to her old man, she's got a chappie, anyway. Some Crown Prince boddo from one of the neighbouring principalities.'

'Whatever loves she may previously have nurtured in her bosom, Blotto, I can assure you that you have now replaced them in her affections . . .'

'Oh, rodents,' he said miserably.

'. . . and I want you to take advantage of your position to find out what she knows about Captain Schtoltz.'

'What, beard her during the pre-prandials, you mean?'

'No, I've spoken to Mummy, and she has rearranged the *placement*. You'll be sitting next to ex-Princess Ethelinde right through dinner.'

'Biscuits,' said Blotto. 'How dashed embarrassing.' Proximity to a filly who had an eye for him always brought Blotto out in the crimps. Still, just have to grin and bear it. Distance, he seemed to recall, brought enchantment to the view, so maybe proximity might do the opposite. Spending more time in his company might take the shine off the ex-Princess's romantic aspirations. 'Incidentally, old bloater,' he went on to Twinks, 'do you know yet who killed the Captain johnnie?'

'No. But I am continuing my enquiries.'

'That's all right then.' It would be. If Twinks was on the case, there'd be no need for any worries.

'I have to speak to Grimshaw. He is going to assist me in the next stage of my investigation.'

'Oh, you'll be all tickey-tockey then. He's a good green-gage . . . well, I mean, considering he's a servant.'

Grimshaw was in his pantry, like a General planning the troop movement that would be dinner. Normally at such moments he dealt sharply with interruptions, but then he always had time for Twinks. Like most men, he was – in spite of his inappropriately humble status – a little in love with her.

She outlined the services she required of him. Grimshaw nodded sagely and said, 'I think it would be prudent to employ Harvey in this matter.'

'Her discretion is unimpeachable?'

40

'Oh, I can vouch for that.' And his tone of voice implied the wink which someone of his demeanour would never have allowed to cheapen his face.

'Excellent, Grimshaw. I will call you in the morning for the relevant information.'

'I will see to it that I am possessed of it by then, milady.'

Conversation at the dinner table that evening was as stilted as a twelve-foot clown. Blotto remembered some chap once telling him some witty tag about guests and cheese smelling after three days. Or was it guests and fish . . . ? Anyway, whichever it was, the line was certainly proving true with the Mitteleuropian party. This was the fourth dinner they'd spent at Tawcester Towers and the supply of conversational topics was running very low. The first night they'd started with family, because, like most English aristocrats, the Lyminsters were related to ex-King Sigismund through a complex spider's web of cousins. They'd started with crowned heads – who'd married whom, which ones had been deposed, which surrendered in bloodless coups, which assassinated.

Then the second night they'd dealt with the topics of hunting and other sports. This had inevitably led to discussion of cricket and the inability of any but the English to understand it properly. Blotto thought he'd been quite amusing during the hour and a half he'd spent explaining the laws of the game. Mind you, he reckoned three of the Mitteleuropian party going to sleep during his exposition had been pretty bad form.

The third night they'd been reduced to that old conversational stand-by, the English weather.

But on the fourth night . . . Everyone was tired after the day in the field – not to mention bloated after their excessive lunch. The dinner table talk stopped and started, puffed and juddered like a Sunday train on the Tawsworthy branch-line. It was enough to make a chap uneasy.

And Blotto's uneasiness was compounded by the way the guest to his right kept fluttering her dark eyelashes at him. He wondered at first whether the ex-Princess was suffering from some kind of nervous tic, but he was rather afraid she wasn't. The eyelash-fluttering was for his benefit.

'Um . . .' said Blotto, falling back on the good old opening gambit which had never let him down before.

'Yes?' asked the ex-Princess eagerly.

'Nothing, really . . . Just "um", actually.'

'Ah.'

Encouraged by this successful ice-breaker – and remembering Twinks's emphasis on the fact that his approach should be made *subtly*, he went on, 'Did you know that Captain Schtoltz had been killed?'

'I beg your pardon?'

Maybe that direct assault had been a bit less subtle than his sister had intended. Blotto backtracked. 'No, sorry, got my words wrong.' Searching desperately for subtlety, he rephrased his previous remark. 'What I meant to say was: "Has it ever occurred to you that Captain Schtoltz might have been killed?"'

The dark brow of the ex-Princess furrowed. 'I do not think so.'

'Well, he isn't here now, is he?'

'No. My father has sent him on a secret mission.'

'Do you know where to?'

'Even if I did know, I could not tell you. I said it was a secret mission.'

'Yes.' For a moment Blotto chewed over this thought, together with a mouthful of excellent local lamb. 'Presumably a secret mission could also be a dangerous mission?'

The ex-Princess shrugged her deliciously slender shoulders. 'Perhaps. Such things – such political things – are man's work.'

'Yes, of course. And you, being a woman – er, I mean a lady – would not be interested in man's work.'

'Not in man's work,' she breathed, 'but in a man, yes.' And her eyelashes went into a routine like two butterflies doing an energetic Charleston.

Blotto didn't think he was going to have that much to report back to his sister. Captain Schtoltz had been sent on a 'special mission' – they already knew that. He spent the rest of the dinner trying once again to explain cricket to ex-Princess Ethelinde. At the end she seemed to have got the laws pretty firmly ensconced in her mind. What she failed to grasp, though, was the point of it all.

Women, thought Blotto.

At the other end of the table, his sister was making rather more progress. She had leant on her mother about her own *placement* at the table, and as a result was seated next to the Margrave von Humpenstaupen, one of ex-King Sigismund's closest aides. Twinks's choice of companion had not been random. She had immediately recognized in the Margrave's eyes the tell-tale signs of infatuation. In her English beaux the symptoms of this common malady were a mouth slightly agape, popping eyes, redness round the collar and a total inability to string two words together. In the Margrave von Humpenstaupen the mouth slightly agape, popping eyes and redness round the collar were coupled with the total inability to stop talking.

But that was fine with Twinks. The main point was that the Margrave von Humpenstaupen was more than ready to fall in love with her. Men in that condition, she knew from experience, were liable to be indiscreet. And indiscretion was what she was after.

While the Margrave prattled at some length about the quality of the hunting at Berkenziepenkatzenschloss, she took the opportunity to observe his moustache. It was indeed a construction of gothic proportions. Seemingly anchored to the face only from two small areas beneath the nostrils, it tapered and curled in black profusion, resembling nothing so much as some abstruse key notation on an ancient musical manuscript. At what system of nets, restraints and guards was used to preserve the moustache while the Margrave slept, Twinks could only conjecture.

During the survey of his facial hair, she became aware that his voluble discourse had moved away from hunting to a subject to which she had become accustomed over the years – her beauty. And, though the topic itself bored her, the Margrave von Humpenstaupen's elaborate Continental flourishes at least made a change from the strangulated compliments she regularly received from her English admirers.

'From classical times . . .' The words rolled grandiloquently off his tongue. 'From classical times, there has always been an ideal of feminine beauty . . . an ideal sought after, bought at great price and fought over. This ideal has for men, since time immemorial, been a kind of Holy Gruel.'

'Grail, I think you mean,' suggested Twinks.

'Grail, yes. Sorry, my English is not always so good. In English I do not have . . . how do you say, "the gift of the gob"?'

'Gab,' said Twinks.

'Gab, yes, of course. But, as I am saying, feminine beauty is something for which men have always striven. To possess the immaculate, to own the perfect – it is for this end that many wars have been fought. Did not Helen of Troy have "the face that launched a thousand chips"?'

'"Ships",' said Twinks.

'Ships, yes. So, as I say, men have always wished for this ideal. I too – I, the Margrave von Humpenstaupen –'

'Yes, I know who you are. We were introduced.'

'I am sorry. I am employing the "emphatic nomenclature". It is a device much used in Mitteleuropian literature.'

'Ah,' responded Twinks, thinking that so far, amongst her wide reading, she had managed to avoid Mitteleuropian literature. And that she might continue to do so. But, even as she had the thought, her diligent mind recognized that reading the literature of the country might help in her continuing studies of its language. She made a mental note to begin climbing the North Face of a Mitteleuropian novel at the earliest opportunity.

'So I too – the Margrave von Humpenstaupen –' the Margrave von Humpenstaupen went on, again using what Twinks now recognized to be Mitteleuropian 'emphatic nomenclature', 'have wished to encounter this ideal of feminine beauty. And, to my surprise, when this transcendental moment comes to me, it is not amid the verdant forests of my homeland, but in England. Here at Tawcester Towers I find the woman who of all feminine beauty is the parasol!'

'I think possibly you mean "paragon",' said Twinks.

'Paragon, yes. And it is you, Lady Honoria, who is that paragon. All the beauty of all the world's women in the past has been building up to one climax, to one high spot of perfection, of which you are the acne.'

'Acme, I think, 'said Twinks. She had by now decided that this cornucopia of compliment needed to be stemmed before he moved on to the declaration stage. The Continentals got so operatic about that kind of thing. She didn't feel up to threats of duels to any other men who dared look at her, or the Margrave's suicide if she did not succumb to his blandishments. 'I would really like to talk to you,' she went on, 'about Captain Schtoltz.'

His demeanour changed instantly, the complexion of his face darkening almost to the hue of his moustache.

'Captain Schtoltz?' he echoed. 'What should I know of Captain Schtoltz?'

'Well, he was with you when your party arrived at Tawcester Towers, and, so far as I can tell, he is no longer with you.'

'Ah.' The Margrave's black pupils moved furtively from side to side, as if trying to escape the confines of their lids. 'The fact is,' he continued, 'that Captain Schtoltz had suddenly to return to Zling, in Mitteleuropia ... er, due to family decomposition.'

'Decomposition?'

'Yes, Lady Honoria. Does not this word mean "illness"?'

'Well, a rather extreme form of illness. I think, Margrave, "indisposition" is perhaps the word you're looking for.'

'"Indisposition", good. Yes, he has returned to Zling, due to family indisposition.'

'You're sure he hasn't been sent there by the ex-King?'

'No, he has gone there of his own occurred.'

'Accord.'

'Accord, right.'

'But won't he be in danger if he returns to Zling?'

'Why?'

'Well, I understood that the country was now under the control of King Vlatislav.'

'He is not the King! Sigismund is the only King of Mitteleuropia! Vlatislav is a usurper!'

'Yes, of course, I'm so sorry,' said Twinks, relieved that this outburst had passed unnoticed in the general conversation of the dinner. 'But what I am saying is that, whatever the health of his family, surely Captain Schtoltz, as a loyal supporter of ex-King – sorry, *King* Sigismund, will be at risk from the forces of King – sorry, the *usurper* Vlatislav . . .?'

'Ah, yes,' said the Margrave von Humpenstaupen slowly. 'Yes. No, I'm sorry. I have this wrong. I am thinking of something else . . . What I meant to say was that Captain Schtoltz has gone to London for an appointment . . .' There was a long silence before he went on, 'He has gone to meet his bootmaker.'

Meet his Maker more likely, thought Twinks. And she reckoned even Blotto would have worked out that the Margrave von Humpenstaupen was lying.

6

An Overheard Conversation

Blotto had mixed feelings when the time came for the ladies to withdraw from the dinner table. On the one hand, he was relieved to be excused the vigorous eyelash-fluttering of ex-Princess Ethelinde. On the other, he didn't find the male company on offer much more attractive. Though fully aware of his duties as an Englishman and a host, he'd really rather had a bellyful of Mitteleuropians and their tedious politics. It was that gag about guests and fish again. Or was it cheese? Something niffy, anyway. Cracks were appearing in Blotto's normally unfailing bonhomie. All he really wanted was a large brandy and soda and the welcome embrace of his single bed.

But the Mitteleuropians still had rituals to perform. There were elaborate post-prandial toasts to be drunk and, to add to the general inconvenience, the guests had introduced their own alcohol. Bottles of a colourless fluid called Splintz were brought forward with great ceremony and the ex-King's entourage waxed lyrical about the quality of the experience his 'British friends' were about to share. This was, they insisted, a very rare occasion.

As though it were liquid gold, measures of Splintz were decanted into small glasses. Then followed an unnecessarily long explanation of Mitteleuropian drinking customs. Time-honoured tradition demanded that Splintz could only be drunk in company – drinking it alone brought bad luck – and it must be accompanied by the appropriate toast. Then, from all around the table there was a cry of '*Zugbash!*' and the contents of the glass were downed in one. To Blotto, the first shot felt as though it had stripped several layers off his tongue and then wallpapered his throat with them.

Gasping, he turned his watery eyes on to the gentleman next to him. 'Just wait for the aftertaste,' his neighbour confided with heavily accented glee.

The aftertaste came. In Blotto's opinion it combined the worst qualities of silver polish and turpentine. And none of their good points.

It wasn't just the taste of the stuff either. Each toast had to be accompanied not only by the cry of '*Zugbash!*', but also by elaborate flourishes of compliment. 'King Sigismund wishes to raise his glass to the Duke of Tawcester, whose beneficence and generosity are famed throughout the world, and whose fine qualities of . . .' (This went on for hours.) 'The Margrave von Humpenstaupen wishes to raise his glass *in absentia* to the ladies of Tawcester Towers, whose perfect beauty is without a flea . . .' Toast followed toast, and all Blotto wanted to do was be in bed until he was woken next morning by his manservant Tweedling with some of the buttered variety.

But *noblesse oblige* . . . He knew what belonged to a scion of the Tawcester dynasty. Over the years members of his family might have hacked up a few rival barons in the battlefield and mutilated the odd serf on the estate, but they had never been less than polite to guests within their home. So, after tedious rounds of ever more elaborate toasts, with the Splintz by now removing layers from his internal organs as well as his mouth, he finally escorted his Mitteleuropian guests to the billiard room.

This cavernous space had been added to Tawcester Towers during the nineteenth-century indoor games boom. And fortunately for Blotto it had been added by the Duke who earned himself the soubriquet of Rupert the Antisocial. Not being a lover of his fellow man, this peer had decreed that the design of the room should incorporate a series of alcoves on either side, each centred on a fireplace, over which was fixed a display of swords and other weapons from the Tawcester family armoury. High-backed leather sofas made these spaces into virtually self-contained units.

So, after the minimum of *politesse* to his now rather gamey guests, it was to one of these alcoves that Blotto stole with a quintuple brandy and the merest dribble of soda (after all that Splintz muck, he needed a proper drink).

Ensconced in his refuge, he found himself, as Duke Rupert the Antisocial had intended, as if in a different room from the babble of the tiresome Mitteleuropians. And, having had a busy day on Mephistopheles, along with two very large and generously alcohol-sluiced meals – not to mention the lethal Splintz – Blotto very quickly fell asleep.

When he awoke, it took him a moment or two to remember where he was. He didn't know what time it was either, but the lamps over the billiard tables had been switched off and the only light came from the dying embers of the large open fires. Blotto was about to stretch his stiffening limbs and take himself off to an overdue appointment with bed, when suddenly he realized that he was not alone in the billiard room.

He could hear two voices in earnest conversation. One spoke English with the guttural accent of the Mitteleuropians, the other with that slackness of vowels which always betrays the lack of private education. Blotto was confused as to why a member of the lower classes should be in the billiard room of Tawcester Towers. He was about to rise from his leathern repose to identify the interloper when he heard from the Mitteleuropian words that froze him to the spot.

'The only way we can achieve what we want is to kidnap her.'

'I'm sure that can be arranged, sir,' said the common person.

'She is heavily guarded when she travels.'

'She may be heavily guarded when she travels, but she's not so heavily guarded when she is a guest at an English country house.'

The Mitteleuropian chuckled at this. 'That is exactly the point, my friend. Here at Tawcester Towers she is thought to be safe.'

It was all Blotto could do to stop himself from shouting out, 'And she is safe! Whoever the she in question may be! Over the centuries guests have always been safe at Tawcester Towers! It is a point of family honour, and always has been. Even when Evil Baron Edmund the Murderous visited Rupert the Vicious during the Wars of the Roses, he was not set upon and slaughtered . . . at least not until he had passed the estate boundary. We Lyminsters have standards!'

But he curbed his tongue. Experience – not to mention Twinks – had taught him that there were times when the instinctive response of an Englishman and a gentleman was not necessarily the right one. Sometimes it paid to play the long game. (As a lover of cricket, he should have known that, anyway – he was used to playing an interminable game.) So he waited to see what further treachery was about to be revealed.

'I cannot emphasize enough,' the rasping foreign voice continued, 'how important it is that no suspicion concerning the abduction attaches itself to me.'

'That is fully understood, sir.'

'Nor – and this is vital – that my brother ever finds out that I have any connection with the crime.'

'That is also understood.'

'My brother's loyalty to ex-King Sigismund borders on the obsessive. He will happily lay down his life for any legitimate member of the Schtiffkohler royal family. His integrity is unimpeachable . . . as mine used to be . . .' There was a reflective silence. '. . . before King Vlatislav showed me the error of my ways . . .' A harsh laugh. '. . . and the colour of his money. If my brother gets wind of what we have in mind, he will not stop short of killing us both to foil our plans.'

'I will see that his plans to foil your plans are foiled.'

'But what if he tries to foil your plans to foil his plans to foil my plans?'

'Don't worry, sir. I have a plan to foil his plans to foil my plans to foil his plans to foil your plans.'

'Good. I like people who think ahead. Yes, I knew I'd got the right man to do this job for me. It is for that reason that the fee you are being paid for your services is so generous.'

'Yes, sir.'

'Do you have a plan for how you will effect the kidnapping?'

'I do. I think it will be easiest if I –'

'Please! I do not wish to know. What I am ignorant of cannot be extracted from me . . . even under torture.'

'As you wish, sir. You may rely on my discretion.'

'I hope, for the money I am paying you, I will get more than discretion.'

'Name what else you require, sir, and it is yours.'

'This I know. But tell me, is there danger that anyone here at Tawcester Towers might become aware of what we are planning?'

'Very little danger, sir. We servants know our place, and it is not a place where independent conjecture or curiosity is encouraged. As for the ducal family, they are not susceptible to imaginative thinking. The Duke himself suffers from the congenital family stupidity, and his younger brother is about as bright as a dead mole at the bottom of a coal mine.'

Here was another moment when Blotto had to curb his natural instinct to detonate.

'But what about his sister? The Lady Honoria? I have heard she is a woman of considerable intelligence.'

'She is, sir. And for that reason I will see to it that I effect

51

the kidnap at a time when she is not present at Tawcester Towers.'

'Good. You seem to have thought of everything.'

'I pride myself on doing that, sir.'

'But remember – if any news of what you are planning leaks out before the job is done, you will pay for your care-lessness with your life.'

'Sir, I never expected anything else. The cost of my life is incorporated in the fee.'

'Excellent. And now I must leave.' There was an element of relish in the Mitteleuropian voice as it continued. 'For me, I think, the night is not yet at an end.'

There was a clicking of heavy boots on the wooden floor of the billiard room, and Blotto realized that the secret conference was over. Rising warily, he peered over the top of his leather sofa, and was in time to see two men exiting the billiard room in different directions.

One was the new footman, Pottinger. Blotto was the last person in the world to be prejudiced, but he knew you should never have trusted anyone with ginger hair.

The other man was tall and blond, dressed in a ridicu-lously begarlanded Mitteleuropian uniform. Someone whose intellect fired on more cylinders than the Right Honourable Devereux Lyminster's might have already deduced from the overheard conversation that he was one of the Grittelhoff brothers. But now even Blotto was in no doubt as to the foreigner's identity. It was a Grittelhoff. Though in the semi-darkness whether it was Bogdan or Zoltan Blotto had no means of knowing.

7

Kidnap Alert

'The trouble is, Twinks, they didn't say who was going to be kidnapped.'

'But they did say it was a she, Blotto, and they did say she was a guest at Tawcester Towers, so that narrows the field down a bit. In fact, if one excludes servants . . .'

'And of course one does exclude servants. What on earth would be the point of kidnapping a servant?' Blotto chuckled at the incongruity. 'I mean, who'd waste money paying a ransom? If a servant went missing, you wouldn't bother sending out a search party, would you? You'd just get another one.'

'Precisely.' Twinks was sitting on the edge of her bed, her perfect form draped in grey silk pyjamas. The Mittel-europian novel she had been reading when Blotto knocked on her door was face-down on the bedside table. 'So,' she mused, 'the only two candidates for the role of victim are ex-Queen Klara and ex-Princess Ethelinde.'

'Toad-in-the-hole!' Blotto murmured in awestruck tones. His wished his mind worked like Twinks's. Give her a couple of random facts and she could instantly build a spoffing great cathedral of logic out of them. Not for the first time, Blotto felt properly humble in the dazzling glow of his sister's brilliance.

'And, of the two, I would put my last petticoat on the ex-Princess.'

'Why?'

'Because, Blotto me old gumdrop, you have to ask yourself: which one of them means more to ex-King Sigismund?'

'Why?' he repeated.

'Because the kidnap must be a way of getting at the ex-King. And from the way he looks at ex-Queen Klara, he clearly doesn't care a tealeaf for her.'

'No, well, people in royal marriages never do, do they?'

'Exactly. Romance in a royal marriage would only cloud the water. In such relationships the best starting point is always mutual loathing. But from the way the ex-King looks at ex-Princess Ethelinde . . . well, you can tell he's got a spot as soft as a marshmallow for her.'

'Yes, I suppose he has.'

'So anyone who wants to put the pressure on ex-King Sigismund has only got to threaten his daughter.'

'But why should anyone want to put the pressure on ex-King Sigismund?'

'Oh, come on, Blotto, press the self-starter on the old brainbox! Didn't you listen to all that toffee he told you at luncheon about how he came to be an *ex*-King?'

'No,' her brother replied truthfully.

'Well, you must have got the gist of it. His brother Vlatislav's done the dirty on him and as a result the two of them are at daggers drawn.'

'Oh, yes, I got that much.'

'So the plot to kidnap ex-Princess Ethelinde must involve someone who's in the pay of the usurper Vlatislav.'

'Ah.' Blotto let this thought embed itself in his mind for a moment. Then he said, 'Except that doesn't work. Because the usurper Vlatislav, stuck in Mitteleuropia, is not going to have dealings with a footman like Pottinger . . .'

'Perhaps not.'

'. . . so that would mean that the person in his pay must be one of the Grittelhoff brothers . . . either Zoltan or Bogdan . . . and it can't be one of them.'

'Why not?'

'Well, because they're in the pay of ex-King Sigismund.'

'Has it never occurred to you, Blotto me old gumdrop, that a person could *pretend* to be in the pay of one employer, while in fact also taking money from that employer's sworn enemy?'

'Rodents!' Her brother whistled. 'Nobody'd be such a stencher as to do that, would they?'

'It has been known.'

'But, honestly . . . Well, I mean . . . That isn't cricket, is it?'

'The Mitteleuropians don't play cricket.'

'No.' Blotto nodded, as a new insight came to him. 'And that explains a lot about them.'

'Now,' said Twinks excitedly, clasping her arms around her silk-pyjama-clad knees, 'since we've got this information, we must see to it that the kidnap attempt is thwarted.'

'Good ticket,' her brother agreed. 'What, so do we call in Chief Inspector Trumbull?'

'Heavens, no. He'd come clumping in like a hippo in hobnails and frighten the conspirators off in two tickles of a trout's tail.'

'Yes.' An idea came to him. In the history of Blotto's life such moments should be remarked on. They were rare. 'I suppose we could just get Grimshaw to sack Pottinger?'

'We can't get involved in affairs below stairs.'

'True. Then what do we do – expose the conspirators' dastardly plan to ex-King Sigismund?'

'No, we don't want to worry the old fish. Besides, it'd put us in a slightly dingy light to suggest that such a rotten intrigue could even be contemplated at Tawcester Towers. We can't make accusations against guests in the house, can we?'

'No, frightfully bad form.' Blotto's noble brow crinkled. 'But if we can't accuse them, how can we stop them?'

'Listen, at the moment Pottinger and whichever Grittelhoff brother it was haven't done anything wrong . . .'

'I don't know. I was pretty vinegared off to hear what they –'

'No, they've *discussed* doing something wrong. As the hosts of one of them, we can't unleash the cavalry until we've actually seen them perpetrating a criminal deed.'

'So ...?' Blotto's face recomposed itself into its usual blankness.

'So ... we let them think no one knows about their plan ... we let them get on with it ... and then, just at the moment they try to kidnap the ex-Princess ... we pounce!'

'Hoopee-doopee!' said Blotto. 'But how do we know when they're going to pounce?'

'They told you.'

'Did they?'

'In the conversation you overheard, yes. Pottinger said he was going to do the deed when I was away from Tawcester Towers.'

'Oh yes, so he did. Well done, Twinks!'

'It is well known in the servant circles that the day after tomorrow I have an appointment with my couturier in Bond Street.'

'So you think that's when the deed will be done?'

'I'd put my last shred of laddered silk stocking on it.'

'Right.' Blotto's impossibly handsome face looked troubled. 'So while you're up in Bond Street, it'll be down to me to catch the stenchers red-handed?'

'No. I think it'll be better if I'm here too.'

'Oh, I agree,' said Blotto. Slowly a troubling thought loomed in his mind. 'I think there might be a bit of a snag there, though. If, when the balloon goes up, you're in Bond Street ... well, you can't be here at the same time. Can you?' he asked, worried lest there might be some unsuspected flaw in his logic.

'No, I certainly can't. Well spotted.' He beamed like a retriever who's just retrieved a plugged pheasant for his master, as his sister went on, 'However, I have a solution.'

'Do you?' Blotto waited, open-mouthed, as he had so many times before, in complete confidence that his sister would come up with the silverware.

'I won't go to Bond Street.'

'Toad-in-the-hole ...' Blotto murmured again. 'That, Twinks, is a masterstroke!'

The following morning Chief Inspector Trumbull was summoned to Tawcester Towers by the Dowager Duchess. Sergeant Knatchbull stayed at Tawsworthy police station, busy dealing with a devilish outbreak of underwear theft from local washing lines.

An air of triumph had settled on the Dowager Duchess's solidly patrician features. The day before she had spoken to the mother of Bertie the Chief Constable, and the freemasonry of aristocratic matriarchs had once again worked its magic. A few reminders from his mother of humiliating incidents – and indeed accidents – during his childhood had quickly shown Bertie Anstruther where his duties lay, and he had rung the Dowager Duchess that morning with the message that she wished to hear.

It was clear from Chief Inspector Trumbull's abashed demeanour that he had also had a call from the Chief Constable.

'So, Trumbull ... I gather you have concluded your investigation into that unfortunate incident of the body in the library ...?'

'Yes, Your Grace.'

'Excellent. And I also gather that you have written a report which you will be sending to the Chief Constable ...?'

'I have not yet completed the report, Your Grace.' Chief Inspector Trumbull was a slow writer. 'Indeed, I had just commenced it when I received Mr Grimshaw's telephone call summoning me here.'

'Well, so long as it's in hand.' Then the Dowager Duchess announced, rather in the manner of someone naming a ship, 'I will also require a copy of the report.'

'I am not sure, Your Grace, that including you in the distribution of the document would accord with the practices recommended by the police authorities in such –'

'You will send me a copy, Trumbull. The Chief Constable assured me that you would.' And Bertie'd better keep to his side of the bargain, she thought with relish, or there might start to circulate some nasty stories of soiled knicker-bockers in the nursery.

Trumbull recognized the appropriate limits of resistance. 'Very good, Your Grace.'

'But since the report is not yet finished, Trumbull, I would be grateful if you could provide me with a quick verbal résumé of its findings.'

Chief Inspector Trumbull swallowed as if there were something distasteful in his mouth, then launched into his prepared speech. 'Tuesday last I was called to Tawcester Towers to investigate the discovery of a dead body in the library. Despite initial indications of foul play, the man was found to have died of natural causes. Since he was recognized by nobody at Tawcester Towers, it was concluded that the dead man must have been a vagrant or itinerant worker who had broken into the house, possibly with burglarious intent. He has accordingly been buried in an unmarked grave, and the case is closed.'

'Excellent,' the Dowager Duchess purred. When it came to murder investigations, there was still something to be said for being a member of the British aristocracy. And when it came to pulling strings, she could weave whole tapestries out of them.

She gave Chief Inspector Trumbull leave to return to Tawsworthy police station, where he could help Sergeant Knatchbull entrap the knicker nicker, while she herself went to berate Loofah further about his tardiness in pro-ducing a male heir. And the Dowager Duchess felt a huge sense of gratified relief that the murder of Captain Schtoltz would be investigated no further.

Little knowing how differently her daughter Twinks viewed the situation.

8

A Murderer Unmasked!

Twinks hadn't told Blotto of her plans. Her brother could sometimes be absurdly chivalrous and if he thought she was about to do something inviting danger he was more than capable of putting his oar in. And Blotto's oar tended to be very large and wielded with an abandon that wouldn't have been approved of by his rowing master at Eton.

But Twinks was determined to occupy the next day by finding out exactly how Captain Schtoltz had died. If, as she suspected, the men Blotto had overheard in the billiard room were responsible for the murder, then, once she'd proved that, she would be better placed to thwart their planned kidnapping of ex-Princess Ethelinde.

Her enquiries would in time necessitate conversation with Grimshaw, but the first part Twinks could do on her own. Up in her bedroom she extracted three large manila envelopes from their hiding place in the lining of the ottoman, and spread the contents of one over the surface of her dressing table. Its mirror reflected the perfect symmetry of her face, the blonde hair that peeped shyly beneath the edges of her cloche hat, but Twinks was unaware of the image that faced her. Someone as beautiful as she had no need for vanity. Besides, she was far too interested in what lay on the table to notice anything else.

She shuffled through the photographs she had taken of

the unfortunate Captain Schtoltz in the library. She had already scanned them many times, but knew that each fresh scrutiny might unearth some detail that had hitherto escaped her. With a silver propelling pencil she entered her observations in a small leatherbound notebook.

When satisfied that the photographs had told her all they could at that moment, she turned to the second envelope. This contained a plan of the upper storey of the part of Tawcester Towers that lay directly above the library. The area had been planned as a self-contained unit, which could effectively be shut off from the rest of the house. The original reason for this design had been to stop Duke Rupert the Unhinged from getting out, but it was equally suitable for preventing unwanted intruders for getting in. It had therefore been ideal for the Mitteleuropian party who, probably reacting to unpleasant experiences in less honourable countries, seemed not to trust the assurances of their safety given by the ducal family. So great was the ex-King's level of paranoia that he would allow none of the Tawcester Towers staff into his private area. (From someone of less elevated status, the Dowager Duchess might have taken exception to this stricture, but at that moment Sigismund was still the rightful King of Mitteleuropia. Should subsequent political events prove this not to be the case, ex-Queen Klara had been left in no doubt by the Dowager Duchess that her family's reception at Tawcester Towers in future might be considerably less indulgent.)

The floor above the library was divided by a broad central corridor. On one side was the lavish suite of rooms occupied by the ex-King, ex-Queen and ex-Princess. Opposite were three less lavish rooms, which had been allotted, one either side to each of the Grittelhoff brothers, and the one in the middle to the unfortunate Captain Schtoltz.

The placing of his accommodation was a measure of the trust which ex-King Sigismund had placed in the murdered man. Schtoltz was part of the inner circle of security with which the usurped monarch surrounded himself. A trusted confidant, despatched on a secret mission, presumably to Mitteleuropia, a man of whose fate Sigismund was still unaware.

After further intense scrutiny of the floor-plan, Twinks moved on to the contents of the third envelope. Taking the precaution first of spreading tissue paper across the table-top, she shook them out. To the casual observer they might have looked like domestic waste, the contents perhaps of a housemaid's dustpan. But to Twinks's informed eyes, each shred and scrap had its own secret to betray.

She listed the items in her notebook. The stub of a match, a flake of tobacco, a carpet fibre, a scraping of white paint, a particle of chalk, a sliver of red leather, a curl of dyed wool. Between these objects and the photographs, Twinks knew she had the entire story of Captain Schtoltz's murder. Everything was there. She had only to find the code that would unlock the enigma.

Against each item she then listed the exact place where it had been found when she had examined the body in the library. The match-stub she had found in Captain Schtoltz's waistcoat pocket; the flake of tobacco had come from the lapel of his jacket. The carpet fibre had been caught in a crevice in the dead man's shoe; the white paint had been scraped off by one of the buttons on his cuff. The particle of chalk had lodged in the engraved initials on his signet ring; the sliver of red leather had been found in his trouser turn-up. And the small curl of dyed wool had been trapped amongst the jewels on the flamboyant insignia pinned to his sash.

Twinks submitted all of the items on the tissue paper to even more detailed inspection. She sniffed at some of them – particularly the curl of wool – and then consulted various weighty tomes that she kept hidden behind the ball dresses in one of her wardrobes.

A murder scenario was taking shape in her head. But there still remained a few missing pieces in her jigsaw of Captain Schtoltz's death. She rang the bell for Grimshaw.

* * *

'As I suggested, I used the services of Harvey, milady.'

'And she was able to find out the information I requested?'

'Indeed.'

'I hope in the course of her investigations she was not obliged to do anything that went against her nature.'

'No, milady. Rather the reverse.'

'So she managed to gain access to the bedrooms of both Grittelhoff twins?'

'Indeed.'

'I am impressed by her skills. Particularly since both of the brothers make their living as bodyguards.'

'Let us say, milady, that Harvey managed to make both of them lower their guards. And, as for their bodies –'

'I don't think it is necessary for me to know all the details, Grimshaw.'

'No, milady.'

'I mentioned that I did not wish either of the Grittelhoff brothers to be aware that the other was also being . . . what shall I say – paid attention? Was Harvey able to achieve that?'

'She was, milady.'

'She is a woman of remarkable skills, Grimshaw.'

'Oh, indeed.' The spectre of a smile crept across the butler's face. 'And considerable versatility.'

'And did she also manage to gain access to the intervening bedroom – the one formerly occupied by Captain Schtoltz?'

'Indeed.'

'And from there she produced the sample I requested?'

Wordlessly, Grimshaw handed over a small envelope.

'And then while she was in the rooms of the two gentlemen . . .'

Grimshaw produced two more envelopes. On one was firmly written the word 'Bogdan', on the other 'Zoltan'.

'Thank you.' Twinks looked down at her prizes with a moment of doubt. 'I hope my conjectures are correct . . .'

'They invariably are, milady.'

'Yes, but in this case . . . I have never before dealt with identical twins. It is possible that in everything, not only their physical characteristics, but also their tastes, there is no distinction to be found between them.'

Grimshaw emitted a small cough of disagreement. Twinks looked at him quizzically. 'According to Harvey, milady, the gentlemen were not identical in *every* way.'

'Oh. Oh.' For a moment Twinks was tempted to ask for more detail of the housemaid's night-time activities. But breeding triumphed over prurience. 'That will be all, thank you, Grimshaw. Could you ask my brother Devereux to join me here?'

'Of course, milady.' And the butler hastened off to fulfil that commission and then to find Harvey. He was enthusiastic to hear all the details of the housemaid's night-time activities. For him, prurience always triumphed over breeding.

Blotto had been pleased to receive Twinks's summons. He wasn't having a great day. The excesses of the night before – particularly the noxious Splintz – had left him with a very woolly morning head and a mouth tasting like a septic tank. But that day none of his normal means of dealing with such a condition were available to him. It wasn't the cricket season. There was no hunting arranged within three counties of Tawcester Towers. And he couldn't even fall back on his customary longstop resource of going out with his Purdey and blasting a few pheasants to blazes. If he wanted to go shooting, honour would demand that he should invite the house's guests, and by the time all the Mitteleuropians had got themselves together – and stopped for meals – he would have gone off the whole idea.

Worse than that, thought Blotto gloomily, I haven't even got an adventure at the moment. Well, he had of course, but Blotto, not being a boddo of very retentive memory, had forgotten all about it. So he was doubly chuffed when

Grimshaw's summons reminded him of the mysterious death of Captain Schtoltz. He zapped post-haste to his sister's dressing room.

'So, old bloater,' he asked on arrival, 'what's the bizz-buzz? Have you pieced the whole rombooley together? Have you fingered our murderer?'

Twinks smiled confidently. 'I'm pretty sure I'm there, yes. Don't know whether the case would stand up in a British court of justice yet, but I can't see good old St Peter letting the stencher into Heaven.'

'So are you going to tell me who it is?'

'No, I am not, Blotto me old gumdrop. You're going to have to listen to how I worked it out first.'

'Oh, all right,' he conceded quickly. He was quite familiar with his sister's modus operandi when she was on a case, and content to be amazed by her brilliance.

'This is what happened on the evening of Captain Schtoltz's death . . .' Twinks still had her scraps of evidence spread out on the tissue paper, and she indicated each one as its role in the story became relevant. 'At about six o'clock he was in his bedroom . . .'

'How do you know it was six o'clock?'

'Because by half-past six all the rest of the Mitteleuropian party were downstairs drinking pre-prandial champagne.'

'Good ticket, Twinks.'

'Captain Schtoltz was, however, himself having a drink in his room.'

'Alone?'

'No.'

'How do you know?'

Twinks pointed to the matchstick stub. 'Do you see how little of this is left?' Her brother nodded. 'If it had only been used to light one cigar it would not have burnt down so far. So clearly it was used to light two. Captain Schtoltz had company.'

'Toad-in-the-hole, Twinks, what a brainbox you are!'

'My conjecture is substantiated by this . . .' She indicated the tiny flake of tobacco. 'The cigar from which this comes is a flamboyantly large one of European manufacture. It is in fact from the type known as a Transcarpathian Emperor, probably bought at Melanevsky's Specialist Tobacco Shop on the Vartlav Parade in Zling. But that is only part of its significance. The flake came from the end of the cigar which Captain Schtoltz had in his mouth – it was slightly damp, which is why it clung to his lapel. And, as well as the characteristic almond smell of the cyanide that killed him, there is on the flake a distinctive aroma of Splintz, suggesting that that was the beverage into which the poison was decanted. And, as I'm sure I don't need to tell you, Blotto, no Mitteleuropian would ever risk the bad luck attendant on drinking Splintz on his own.'

'So there was some other boddo with him . . .?'

'Definitely.'

'Who?'

Twinks raised her hand to stop his questions. She was going to spell out her conclusions at her own pace, and didn't want to miss out any step in her tortuous journey of logic.

'The cyanide would have killed Captain Schtoltz almost immediately –'

'Just a sec, Twinks me old muffin. How can you be sure that the poor pineapple was killed in his own bedroom?'

'Look at these.' She indicated two pieces of carpet fibre on her tissue paper. One she had removed from the crevice in the murder victim's shoe. The other was the sample that Harvey had extracted, according to instructions, from the room used by Captain Schtoltz.

'Both pieces, as you can see, are from the same carpet. It's a Turkish fine-weave, probably manufactured in the workshop of the Hassan brothers in the village of Akgürglu just to the north of Izmir, and almost definitely originally bought from the emporium of their cousin Mustapha Khalid on the Golden Alley of the main Istanbul souk. Not that any of that's important. The important thing is that both samples came from the same carpet.'

'But surely,' said. Blotto, relishing one of those wonderful, rare moments when he actually saw a flaw in his sister's reasoning, 'if the poor old thimble had been staying in the room for a couple of days, there's no great surprise to find a bit of the carpet on his shoe?'

'It is not the simple fact that it's from the same carpet that's important,' said Twinks evenly. 'It is the smell on the sample from his shoe that defines both the timing and the place of his murder.'

'Ah.' Blotto was deflated. In retrospect, he comforted himself, it really had been too good to be true, the thought of catching his sister out when it came to a matter of investigation.

'This fibre smells of Splintz, so it must have been picked up at the moment of the victim's death, when some of his drink was spilled during the convulsions which the cyanide would have sent through his body.'

'Ah,' said Blotto. 'Right.'

'So,' Twinks continued magisterially, 'Captain Schtoltz was poisoned in his bedroom. His body was then manhandled to the window, against whose ledge a button of his jacket scraped ...' She pointed to another of her exhibits. '... dislodging *this* flake of white paint. The dead man was dropped to the flowerbed, where I found indentations made by his falling body, and where the engraving on his signet ring picked up *this* particle of chalk.

'His murderer then went downstairs to the library, opened the french windows and dragged the body inside, during which process the Captain's trouser turn-up gathered *this* sliver of leather, which had flaked off the binding of one of the books in the shelves above. In fact, the book from which the sliver came was Tacitus's *De origine et situ Germanorum*.

'Captain Schtoltz's body was then left by the murderer in the middle of the library floor ... where, Blotto me old gumdrop, you found it.'

Twinks smiled with satisfaction, as if her narrative were

complete. Her brother fell for the tease and asked with some desperation, 'So who *was* the murderer?'

'Oh yes, of course,' said Twinks, as though she had genuinely forgotten to supply that detail. Then she pointed to the curl of dyed wool that had been found trapped in the jewelled insignia on Captain Schtoltz's chest. '*Here* is the clue that answers that question for us. This also smells of Splintz, not to mention cyanide, so we know that it was trapped at the moment of the victim's death. Reconstructing that moment, I would estimate that, as Captain Schtoltz realized that he had been poisoned, he leapt forward to attack his killer. It was then that his jewelled insignia snagged on the murderer's uniform, detaching this curl of wool. The fabric is a blue woollen twill supplied by the tailors Grünbaum & Pesch of Kathedralstrasse in Zling ... an emporium patronized by the Grittelhoff brothers.'

'So it *was* one of them!' said Blotto gleefully.

'Yes.'

'But which one?'

Twinks again indicated the curl of wool. 'As well as the smells of Splintz and cyanide, there is a third aroma on this shred of fabric. That of a man's cologne.'

'Yes, I noticed the Grittelhoffs use cologne. Filthy Continental habit! I always think that men should smell like men.'

'I'd noticed that, Blotto.'

'But there's a bit of a chock in the cogwheel, Twinks, because both of the stenchers use the rotten skunk-juice, so how can you know –?'

Twinks raised her hand for silence. 'Yes, they both use cologne, but they do not use the *same* cologne.' She indicated the scented handkerchiefs which Harvey had managed to extract from the two men's rooms. 'This is Vol de Nuit, manufactured by the parfumier Nicholas Rodette of the Champs Elysées in Paris ... while *this* is Der Jäger, a fragrance sold exclusively by the Bonetti Barbershop at 417 Hedwigstrasse in Zling.'

Blotto was almost panting by now. 'So which is the cologne on the spoffing bit of wool? And which twin uses the spoffing stuff?'

'The cologne on the bit of wool is Der Jäger.' Twinks spoke slowly, relishing her revelation. 'And the Grittelhoff brother who uses it is Bogdan.'

'So he's our murderer? Bogdan Grittelhoff killed Captain Schtoltz?'

'Definitely,' said his sister.

'Toad-in-the-hole, Twinks, you are absolutely the lark's larynx!'

9

Plans Afoot

Some people might have been tempted at this point to go to the police with their information and have Bogdan Grittelhoff arrested for the murder of Captain Schtoltz. Then no doubt in time Pottinger could also have been arrested for plotting the kidnap of ex-Princess Ethelinde.

This course of action, however, would have failed to take into consideration two important facts. One, it would go against every instinct of Twinks and Blotto as amateur investigators to bring in professional outsiders before the case was entirely sewn up. And two, the police in Tawcestershire were represented by Chief Inspector Trumbull and Sergeant Knatchbull. The chances of those two actually arresting the right people were so slender as to be negligible.

So Twinks recommended a watching brief. The following day was the one when she was supposed to be going to Bond Street to visit her couturier, and it was then that Bogdan Grittelhoff and Pottinger were planning to seize the ex-Princess. So she made plans for the following day, and spelled them out in detail to Blotto.

His part of the preparations was one that appealed to him. He had to go to the Tawcester Towers garages, and he always got a positive buzz from the atmosphere of the place. The cars themselves were pretty impressive – the Rolls-Royces, the Hispano-Suizas and his own personal favourite, which was one of the Lagondas. If some scientist johnnie ever managed to cross a tiger with a gazelle, then Blotto reckoned the resulting offspring would be pretty like the Lag. The car was brimming with personality and he always felt he read some personal message in the gaze of its huge headlamps. Hurtling the machine round blind corners of country lanes at speeds over a hundred brought Blotto almost the same thrill as hunting. In the latter scenario a fox was the quarry, in the former local peasants. Both experiences were exhilarating. In a car like the Lag, which got through fuel like a dipsomaniac on champers, a man really felt at one with nature.

The other great attraction of the garages was that it gave Blotto a chance to speak to Corky Froggett. Corky wasn't the senior chauffeur at Tawcester Towers, but he was the most important one. In the army he'd been a driver (as well as many other unspeakable things – in fact he was a highly trained killing machine), and his bearing was still military. His thickset, heavily muscled body pressed against the restraint of the black buttons on his black uniform, his high black boots were soldier's boots, and he wore his black peaked cap as though it had a regimental badge on it. His face was the red of a Buckingham Palace guardsman, and a white moustache stood to attention beneath his cavernous nostrils. He gave the impression that all the other unseen hairs on his body were also standing to attention.

'Ah, milord,' he said as Blotto approached. His accent was all jellied eels and pearly kings. 'What a pleasure to see you. Do you wish me to get the Lagonda into battle trim?'

'No, not driving today, Corky. The Mater doesn't want me too far off the prems while these spoffing Mitteleuropians are still around. Must say, I'm beginning to find a little of them goes a long way.' There was still a dull ache around his temples from the Splintz of the night before. 'Something about guests and garlic ... or is it guests and cheese ...?'

'I'm sure you're right, milord.'

'Do you like Mitteleuropians, Corky?'

'To the best of my knowledge I've never killed any. So my initial inclination would be to give them the benefit of the doubt.'

'Oh, good ticket. Very right and proper. As British people, "the benefit of the doubt" is the absolute minimum we should offer to . . . boddos like that. A lot of them are complete charmers. It's just their bad luck to be born foreign.'

'Yes, milord.'

'Mind you, after three days, guests and . . . onions, was it?' But the precise phrasing did not come back to him, so Blotto moved on. 'They've presumably got cars with them, have they?'

'Yes.' Corky Froggett's moustache bristled with distaste. 'Four of those big Krummel-Laportes – built like tanks, drive like tanks. Three Basgatis and a couple of Frimmel-stopf roadsters.'

Blotto was instantly alert. 'Oh, they're pretty hot from the chocks, the Frimmelstopfs, aren't they?'

Corky's head shook dismissively. 'In the Lagonda you'd burn 'em off in half a mile – and still have time to mani-cure your fingernails.'

'Hm . . .' A distant longing came into Blotto's eyes. 'Wouldn't mind having a go at that one day . . .'

'Maybe it can be arranged, milord.'

'Maybe . . .' He shook himself out of his reverie. 'Actually, what I've come to see you about, Corky, is a trip you're slated in to do tomorrow . . .'

'That would be driving the Lady Honoria to London, would it not?'

'It would indeed. Now the thing is . . . I can rely on your discretion, can't I?'

'Were you to entrust me with a secret, milord, I would not reveal it if hot coals were sprinkled liberally over my extremities. I would not reveal it if my finger- and toenails were extracted one by one. I would not reveal it if red-hot branding irons were used to write the entire Sanskrit alphabet on the most sensitive parts of my anatomy. I would not reveal –'

'All right, Corky, thought I could rely on you. I don't think you'll actually have to go through any of all that, but . . .' Blotto thought briefly about what he had witnessed so far of the character of the Mitteleuropians. 'Well, I suppose you might . . .'

'It would be an honour, sir. And I guarantee your secret would remain intact.'

'Very glad to know it. Now, as you say, Twinks is going up to Bond Street tomorrow to visit the old rag-stitcher, and I dare say what you'd normally do is get one of the Rolls-Royces spick and span, then drive it round to the front entrance of the Towers to pick her up . . .?'

'That, I can confirm, is what I would normally do, milord.'

'Right. Well, tomorrow I want you to do something slightly different . . .'

The first part of the following day's plan went like clockwork. Twinks appeared at breakfast wearing a deliciously short dress in salmon pink and made a great point of talking to the Mitteleuropian party about her forthcoming visit to Bond Street. She discussed with ex-Queen Klara and ex-Princess Ethelinde the relative merits of London and Paris as centres of fashion, and ensured that this conversation was conducted within the hearing of the Grittelhoff brothers. By now she had studied the two closely enough to be able to tell them apart (without recourse to Harvey's more intimate knowledge). Zoltan had the vestige of a scar – no doubt from duelling – that bisected his right eyebrow, whereas Bogdan – or as she and Blotto now thought of him, *the murderer* – had a small mole on the lobe of his left ear.

Then, with great ceremony, Twinks had put on her outdoor pale green coat and hat, said goodbye to her mother and brother and set off down to the garages. She had elected to walk because it was another lovely autumn day and she wanted to spend as little time as possible confined in the automobile.

Corky Froggett was fully prepared for her arrival and welcomed her loudly at the gate of the garage which contained the day's Rolls-Royce. 'All ready to go up to *London*, milady? It's a very nice day for going up to *London*. I'm sure you'll have a great time in *London*.' This emphasis was for the benefit of the two Mitteleuropian chauffeurs who were in earshot, polishing the silver bonnets of the gleaming Frimmelstopf roadsters, whose tops were down and whose leather upholstery was warming quietly in the autumn sun.

'Yes, certainly ready for *London*,' Twinks agreed, in case the chauffeurs had not yet got the point.

'Then to *London* we shall go,' said Corky, and led her into the dark recesses of the garage.

Two minutes later he was at the wheel of the Rolls-Royce which proceeded regally out on to the driveway. In the back sat a figure dressed in the unmistakable pale green coat and hat of Lady Honoria Lyminster. The two Mitteleuropian chauffeurs watched her pass, both thinking disloyally that she was even prettier than ex-Princess Ethelinde.

At the window of the loft above the garage Twinks, now dressed in a housemaid's uniform, stood beside her brother watching the outline of the Rolls-Royce diminish down the drive.

'Now listen, Blotto me old gumdrop, we've really got to be on our toes. Bogdan Grittelhoff was planning to snatch the ex-Princess as soon as I was off the premises. So far as he's concerned, I now am. And I think he'll be getting that message very soon.' As if to illustrate her words, one of the Mitteleuropian chauffeurs detached himself casually from his Frimmelstopf roadster and set off on his way back to the main house.

'So what we have to do is to watch everyone like hawks.

Particularly the Grittelhoff brothers, ex-Princess Ethelinde and the corrupt footman Pottinger.'

'Right you are, Twinks me old muffin, neither of my eyes will be left unpeeled.' He picked up a pair of binoculars. 'And through these I'll be able to see which brother it is. Zoltan's the one with the duelling scar on his eyebrow, and Bogdan's got the mole on his earlobe. And I have got this right, haven't I? Zoltan Grittelhoff is the *good* brother, so if I see him with ex-Princess Ethelinde, then he's protecting her, ready to defend her with his life . . .?'

'Well done, Blotto.'

'. . . but if I see Bogdan Grittelhoff, *the murderer*, with ex-Princess Ethelinde, then I challenge the stencher and stop him in his evil tracks?'

'You've ponged it right on the nose.'

'Good ticket.'

'Now you stay up here. The only way Bogdan Grittelhoff is going to get out of Tawcester Towers fast enough to escape pursuit is by using one of those . . .' Twinks pointed down to the Frimmelstopf roadsters. 'So if you see Bogdan Grittelhoff go near the cars, you wrap the Lagonda firmly around yourself and give chase. Is it ready?'

'Certainly is. In the other garage underneath us. Corky Froggett's got the old girl tuned like a Stradi . . . you know, one of those violin romboolies. The Lag's as keen to get moving as a Derby winner in a horse box.'

'Grandissimo! So, while you watch here, I'll station myself in the library . . . you know, that alcove where you can see everyone coming and going through the hall. And if I see Bogdan Grittelhoff with ex-Princess Ethelinde, I'll cling to them like a leech that lost its mother at an early age. Oh, larks! This is going to be fun!'

'Hoopee-doopee, Twinks!'

She slipped back into the big house unnoticed. There was always quite a turnover of housemaids at Tawcester Towers, so the sight of an unfamiliar face below stairs was

74

no novelty. And above stairs no one noticed housemaids anyway (except, as has been mentioned before, certain brandy-fuelled male guests after dinner).

To make her cover even more effective, Twinks had taken a leaf out of Harvey's book and carried a feather duster to present the illusion of purpose in her actions.

The library alcove which she targeted she had known from childhood. One particular chair gave an unrivalled view of the front door, but allowed the watcher to remain unseen. She had sometimes watched from there when her father's mistresses used to slip out of the house in the early hours.

Had the chair not been invisible from the hall, perhaps someone else would have noticed the figure already seated there when Twinks arrived that morning. As it turned out, she was the one who made the discovery.

He was a man in black, pinned to the chair's leather upholstery by a dagger through his heart.

10

Hot Pursuit

Blotto was suddenly aware of activity down by the Frimmelstopf roadsters. One of the chauffeurs rose from his seat on the running board, stubbed out his cigarette and stood to attention as his superiors arrived. Blotto focused his binoculars on the approaching couple.

It was one of the Grittelhoff brothers! With ex-Princess Ethelinde! On the very day for which the kidnap had been planned!

But concern quickly gave way to reassurance as the binoculars found the tall man's eyebrow, which was neatly bisected by an old duelling scar. Zoltan, the good brother. And doing his duty as a bodyguard. The man opened the passenger door (and not for the first time Blotto thought how inconvenient it must be for Continentals to have everything in their cars on the wrong side). The ex-Princess was ushered ceremoniously into her seat. She really looked astonishingly pretty, as scrumptious as a cream tea in a Cornish café. In fact, although Blotto was usually immune to any kind of sentimental guff, that morning she put a flutter into his step and a skip into his heart. She had all the innocence of a mayfly landing on a glassy expanse of water, little knowing that there might be a socking great sea-trout lurking just below the surface.

But at least she was in safe hands. From his eyrie, Blotto heard Zoltan Grittelhoff say, 'So, to the south coast it is,

Your Royal Highness', and the ex-Princess's ready smile confirmed that she was under no coercion. The trip in the car was being taken voluntarily. Had she been with Bogdan Grittelhoff, Blotto would have already been down there, challenging the kidnapper to release his prey. But the ex-Princess was in no danger; Zoltan was protecting her. The Mitteleuropian bodyguard sat in the driving seat, waiting while his chauffeur turned the starting handle, and Blotto watched with satisfaction, as the open-topped Frimmel-stopf roadster kicked up the gravel on its way to safety, out of the Tawcester Towers estate.

Zoltan Grittelhoff was doing the prudent thing. He was getting his charge away from danger. Blotto felt relieved. He would only have to take action if he saw Bogdan Grittelhoff or Pottinger setting off in pursuit of Zoltan's Frimmelstopf roadster.

He had just reached this comforting conclusion when someone burst into his refuge beneath the rafters.

Twinks had raised the odd eyebrow as she hurtled through the Tawcester Towers Main Hall on her way back to the garages. Though housemaids with feather dusters were normally invisible to the upper classes, to see one running (except from a brandy-fuelled male guest after dinner) was something of a rarity.

But Twinks was completely unaware of the effect she was producing. Her only thought was to let her brother know as soon as possible what she had found in the library.

She erupted into the loft of the garages like an ocean liner pursued by torpedoes. Blotto just had time to register the thought that it was rare to see a housemaid with a feather duster in such a state of agitation, before Twinks shouted out, 'The flares have been released! Action stations and all hands on deck! The evil Grittelhoff has declared his hand! The balloon's gone up!'

'Sorry, Twinks,' said Blotto. 'I haven't a clue what you're talking about.'

'I'm talking,' said his sister, 'about another murder!'

'Oh, biscuits,' said Blotto, 'I hope you're telling me it's only a servant. I hope you're not going to say it's another of these spoffing Mitteleuropians.'

'As it happens, it is not another of what you insist on calling "the spoffing Mitteleuropians". But it is one of their confederates.'

'Sorry?'

'The treacherous footman Pottinger has been impaled by a dagger in the library!'

'Who by?' asked Blotto. Then, remembering that he had been at Eton, he amended his question to, 'By whom?'

'It can't have been anyone other than Bogdan Grittelhoff. The two conspirators must've fallen out over their kidnap plans. Bogdan killed Pottinger and is now set on snatching the ex-Princess on his own. Where is the poor girl?'

'On that I can set your mind at rest, Twinks me old muffin. Ex-Princess Ethelinde is in the safe hands of the loyal Zoltan Grittelhoff. He has just taken her off for a drive in one of the Frimmelstopf roadsters. And I must say the young greengage was looking very much as if she had just found out she had a Sunday birthday – not only blithe and bonny, but also distinctly good and gay. No, she's fine – or she will be so long as we don't see Bogdan Grittelhoff coming down here, covered in Pottinger's blood, to get into the other Frimmelstopf roadster and set off in hot pursuit.'

Even as he spoke, Twinks moved to the window and looked down. True to her brother's imagining, Bogdan Grittelhoff, his brow knitted in fury, was hurrying towards the remaining Frimmelstopf roadster. To add to the horror, the front of his uniform was liberally daubed with blood (though whether it had actually come from the fatal wounds of Pottinger, whose blood group was extraordinarily rare, even Twinks couldn't tell . . . well, not at that distance).

'Look, Blotto!'

'Rodents! The bounder's going after them!'

As if once again to illustrate Blotto's words, Bogdan Grittelhoff – who they now thought of as *the double murderer* – was already swinging the Frimmelstopf roadster's starting-handle.

'Is the Lag ready?' asked Twinks urgently.

'Ready as a rare rump on a griddle,' Blotto replied, as the pair of them clattered down the wooden stairs to the garage below.

Bogdan Grittelhoff had got a lead on them and was almost out of the Tawcester Towers gates before the Lagonda's self-starter galvanized the beautiful machine into action. But Blotto was confident. He trusted Corky Froggett's evaluation of the two cars' relative merits.

They were well into the outskirts of Tawsworthy before the Mitteleuropian realized he was being followed. His reaction had a profound effect on that demure little county town. Generations after, stall-holders' descendants would regale their grandchildren with tales of the great Market Day Race. They would describe how fruit and vegetables had been sent flying in every direction, sheep and cattle been terrified into stampeding by the roar of the competing engines. Tawsworthy Abbey had survived the Dissolution of the Monasteries more or less intact, but the front wing of the Frimmelstopf roadster took a large bite out of one of its flying buttresses. And the statue of St Sexburga, famous for her modesty, had its skirt ripped off by one of the Lagonda's hub caps.

In the narrow streets of the town, the Frimmelstopf proved more manoeuvrable that Blotto's gargantuan machine, and by the time they left the debris of Tawsworthy behind them, Bogdan Grittelhoff had considerably increased his lead.

But on the open road, the Lagonda flared its metaphorical nostrils, rather as Mephistopheles did at the beginning of a day's hunting, and started to wolf down the tarmacadam between pursuer and quarry. Blotto and Twinks, the wind rippling through their blond hair and excitement glowing in their cheeks, both looked impossibly handsome.

They had to slow down as the road took them through Little Grudging, but the other side of the town, the Lagonda really opened up, and its front bumper was soon alongside the driver's door of the Frimmelstopf, as the cars careered by at well over a hundred miles an hour. Other road users just had to get out of their way, and the roadside fields were littered with the wreckage of hay wains, brewers' drays and milkmen's floats which just hadn't been quick enough to take evasive action.

'Give up, Grittelhoff!' shouted Blotto. 'Stop the car and take your medicine, or I'll have to force you off the road!'

'You cannot stop me, Englishman! I have a duty to perform! And I will use any means to see that it is performed!'

Suddenly the Mitteleuropian had a gun in his hand.

'Oh, how typical,' said Blotto. 'I might have known you wouldn't fight fair.'

'All is fair in the service of the King!' cried Bogdan Grittelhoff, as the two cars sped along, and an elderly vicar on a bicycle was sent flying into a field.

'Actually,' said Twinks, 'technically the King you serve is not the rightful King, so any duty –'

But the man with the bloodied front seemed to have no interest at that moment in the niceties of the Mitteleuropian constitutional situation. Instead he sighted along the barrel of his pistol.

'Don't you dare shoot my sister,' said Blotto. 'Shoot me by all means, but don't let's bring women into this.'

Bogdan Grittelhoff grinned wickedly and lowered the aim of his gun. He fired two quick shots into the Lagonda's front tyre.

As Blotto fought to control the huge car slithering across the roadway, he had a last sight of the Frimmelstopf's diminishing backview and heard the triumphant laugh fading in his ears. Soon, as the Lagonda slewed to an uneven halt, the Mitteleuropian and his roadster were out of sight.

'What a slimy stencher,' said Blotto despondently. 'He's dumped us well and truly in the gluepot.'

'What do you mean?'

'I mean, Twinks me old muffin, that friend Grittelhoff has quit the scene, leaving us with not even a whiff of his cologne. And we have no hope of catching him.'

'Why not?'

'Because,' her brother explained patiently, 'we are in the middle of the English countryside and, beautiful though that undoubtedly is, it's not terribly well equipped with telephones. So I'll have to walk back to Little Grudging to find one in some hotel or something, then ring the Towers and, quite honestly, by the time Corky Froggett has got the message and come out here and changed the wheel ... well, Bogdan Grittelhoff will have snatched the ex-Princess and be halfway across the Channel with her.'

'Are you saying, Blotto, that you can't change a wheel yourself?'

'Of course not. That's not the kind of thing boddos built in the heroic mould like me do. And it wouldn't be fair on the servant classes if we did. They'd get very vinegared off if we started going round changing wheels for them. They'd lose all sense of purpose.' A new thought struck him. Well, no, 'struck' is probably too speedy a word. Thoughts tended to lumber up to Blotto and nudge him. 'Why? You're not telling me that you can change a wheel, are you?'

'Of course.'

'Toad-in-the-hole, Twinks, you are modern.'

It was a matter of moments for her to produce a set of silk overalls from her reticule and envelop her housemaid's uniform in them, while Blotto removed the spare wheel from its housing. Twinks showed him where to find the Lag's jack and tool-box (something Corky Froggett had always done for him in the past), and then pointed out to him which implements she needed passing to her.

Within four minutes the new wheel was on and the old bullet-shredded one chucked into the dicky. Twinks, pristine clean and maid's uniform unruffled once she'd removed her overalls, whooped, 'Right, on we go!'

Blotto stood irresolute beside the Lagonda. 'You wouldn't like to drive?' he asked pathetically.

The question stopped his sister in her tracks. 'Why?'

'Well, you seem to do everything else better than me . . .'

'Don't be a prize cauliflower, Blotto. The only things I do better than you are things that involve intelligence. When it comes to driving . . . or hunting . . . or playing cricket . . . well, they're really your size of pyjamas. There's no one to touch you.'

The customary broad beam resettled about Blotto's god-like features. 'Thanks, Twinks,' he said as he resumed his position in the driver's seat. 'Now the question is: where has the dastardly Grittelhoff gone?'

'Not too much of a stumper. You overheard Zoltan Grittelhoff say he was taking the ex-Princess to the south coast. Bogdan Grittelhoff's sole aim is to kidnap the ex-Princess, so to the south coast he will have gone in pursuit of his brother.'

'You know, Twinks, if they put what's in your brain in bottles, nobody'd be able to afford to buy them.'

'Oh, what guff, Blotto! Come on, get that self-starter self-starting!'

He did as instructed, and the Lag leapt forward like a puma that's just drawn a bead on a lackadaisical llama. The route to the south coast was pretty straightforward. The main road led through the towns of Tittling, Tattling, Carping and Prattling, in each of which the residual shock on the faces of bystanders informed them that the Frimmel-stopf roadster was only a little way ahead. They were on the right track and, with the thrill of the chase, the Lag went even faster. The autumn afternoon dwindled into evening, as the car ravenously gulped down the miles.

But it had to screech to a halt when, the clifftops of the south coast almost in view, the road divided. They were just north of the seaside town of Smattering, and the sign-post at the junction offered the alternatives of 'Smattering Beach' and 'Smattering Harbour'.

'What do we do now, Twinks?'

'I think we'll have to ask someone.'

'We can't ask anyone. We're in the middle of nowhere. There's nobody about.'

'Don't you believe it. In my experience, it's at moments like this that you're most likely to come across an idiosyncratic but basically lovable rustic eyewitness.'

Even as she spoke, out of the gloaming, from behind a dilapidated cowshed near the signpost, there appeared an idiosyncratic but basically lovable rustic eyewitness. His face was as wrinkled as an over-wintered Cox's Orange Pippin, he wore a grubby sun-bleached smock, and, through his haystack beard, a long piece of straw dangled from his toothless mouth.

'Ooh-arr,' he ruminated in a voice as deep and rich as caramel toffee, 'youm beem gentreed folks from oop citi-fied ways, doan't ee?'

'Excuse me,' said Twinks.

'Ooh-arr, me foine ladyfied gentrywooman, wocken Oi doo fur 'ee?'

'Could you please not talk in dialect?'

'Whoay noither?'

'Some people find it terribly irritating.'

'Oh, all right,' said the idiosyncratic but basically lovable rustic eyewitness, adopting received pronunciation. 'What can I do for you?'

'My brother and I want to know if you've seen a foreign car drive this way?'

'What kind of car would that be? A Frimmelstopf roadster?'

'Exactly right.'

'Well, no, I haven't seen one.'

'If you haven't seen one,' asked Blotto, 'then why, of all the cars in the known universe, did you ask if we were looking for a Frimmelstopf roadster?'

'I said I haven't seen one.' The rustic shifted his piece of straw from one side of his mouth to the other. 'I've seen *two*.'

'Each one driven at high speed by an identical twin?'

'Yes, milady, exactly right.'

'And did either of them also have a young woman travelling as a passenger?'

'Oh yes.'

'So which one?' asked Blotto desperately.

'The one that had a young woman travelling as a passenger was the first one that drove past at high speed.'

'Zoltan,' murmured Twinks.

'And the second one contained only a driver.'

'Bogdan,' murmured Twinks.

'And if you want closer identification,' said the obliging rustic, 'the driver of the first Frimmelstopf roadster had an old duelling scar bisecting his right eyebrow, and the driver of the second Frimmelstopf roadster had a small mole on his left earlobe.'

'It must be them!' cried Blotto. 'Or two people who're very good at disguise!'

'But which way did they go?' demanded Twinks.

'Ah, milady, I would have thought someone with a deductive intellect like yours could have worked that out for yourself.'

'What do you mean?'

'Well, in a kidnap situation, where an individual is planning to abduct an ex-Princess and take her to the Continent, given the choice of "Smattering Beach" and "Smattering Harbour", don't you think most people –?'

'Smattering Harbour!' Twinks exclaimed.

'Exactly right, milady. And now, if you'll excuse me, I do have other people to tell what I've eyewitnessed and point in the right direction.'

'Yes, of course.'

And the idiosyncratic but basically lovable rustic eyewitness again disappeared into the gloaming behind the dilapidated cowshed.

'What a helpful man,' said Blotto, as he targeted the Lagonda like a missile down the narrow lane signposted 'Smattering Harbour'.

On the edge of the sea wall stood a tar-covered fisherman's shack. Outside it untidily, as though parked in haste, stood two Frimmelstopf roadsters, steam still rising from their gleaming bonnets. Just as Blotto and Twinks's Lagonda arrived on the scene, they heard from inside the shack the sound of a gunshot.

11

The Tale of a Twin

The space inside was gothically draped with hanging fishing nets and smelt, to Blotto's nose, like fish (or was it guests?) who had outstayed their welcome by some months. The only illumination came from an ancient oil lamp hooked to a convenient rafter. This trickled a watery light on to a long figure in a black uniform, crumpled into a broken-backed chair, and caught the gleam of the fresh blood that pumped from his chest.

'It's Bogdan,' murmured Twinks. 'Can't you see that the blood that's pouring out of him is a different blood group from what is already caked on to the front of his uniform?'

'No,' murmured Blotto.

The tall bodyguard turned at the sound of their voices. 'Ah,' he said in a voice out of whose sides air seemed to be leaking. 'So you have caught up with me?'

'Yes,' replied Blotto. 'And we are glad to see that your crimes have been discovered and your dastardly plans foiled.'

'I do not understand what you mean.'

'It's quite simple,' said Twinks coolly. 'Do you deny that you poisoned Captain Schtoltz?'

'No, I do not deny it.'

'And that this morning you stabbed to death the treacherous footman Pottinger.'

'I did that as well, yes.'

'Well then,' said Blotto, 'you must understand what I mean. Your crimes have been discovered and your dastardly plans foiled.'

'I do not understand,' the bleeding man wheezed, 'what dastardly plans you are talking about.'

'Do you deny,' Twinks demanded implacably, 'that you have driven down here to the south coast in pursuit of your brother Zoltan and the ex-Princess Ethelinde?'

'I do not deny that either. My brother Zoltan is my sworn enemy. He opposes everything I believe in.' He looked down at the blood bubbling merrily out of his chest. 'It is he who has done this to me.'

'Well,' said Blotto, 'I know it doesn't do to hit a chap when he's down, but I do have to say that I think your brother has done the world a service.'

'No, he has not! Zoltan is a traitor! What he has done has struck at the heart of the Kingdom of Mitteleuropia.'

'Wouldn't you say,' asked Twinks coolly, 'that killing Captain Schtoltz and Pottinger were also acts that struck at the heart of the Kingdom of Mitteleuropia?'

'No, I am a patriot! Everything I have done has been in the service of the King of Mitteleuropia!'

'Ah yes, but which King? There seem to be at least two contenders for that title.'

'There is only one true King of Mitteleuropia!'

Twinks shook her head sagely. 'The supporters of the opposing faction say exactly the same thing.'

'Listen –'

'No, you listen, please, Bogdan Grittelhoff! I want to tell you about your crimes and the reasons why you committed them.'

'Why?'

'Because it is something I usually do at this stage of the proceedings.'

'But I am bleeding to death.'

'Oh, don't worry, I won't go into all the details. Right, listen carefully. Though you have the job of bodyguard to ex-King Sigismund, you have always –'

'But I do not –'

Twinks raised a patient hand. 'Please let me finish. Though you are his bodyguard, you are in fact in the pay of the vile usurper King Vlatislav. Since ex-King Sigismund's deposition you have been sailing under false colours. You will do anything to prevent the restoration of ex-King Sigismund to his birthright, the throne of Mitteleuropia. So, when the ex-King despatched Captain Schtoltz on a secret mission to help his cause, you prevented that mission from being fulfilled by poisoning the messenger. Then you plotted with the treacherous Pottinger to kidnap ex-Princess Ethelinde. But you fell out with your co-conspirator, probably because he demanded money to stop him revealing your plans – the footman class is always doing that kind of thing – and stabbed him to death. Then you drove down here to snatch the ex-Princess Ethelinde from the protection of your honest and honourable brother Zoltan. But he, I am glad to say, has foiled your evil intentions by shooting you.' There was a long pause, and then Twinks asked the question she always enjoyed asking in these circumstances. There is nothing so gratifying for an amateur sleuth as that moment when the criminal admits that you've sewn up the whole case. 'So am I right?'

'No,' Bogdan Grittelhoff gasped. 'You are completely wrong!'

'Well, you would say that. Lying's part of being a stencher like you.'

'You listen to me now, milady.' The dying Mitteleuropian's manner was so authoritative that Twinks was silent. 'You think I planned to kidnap Her Royal Highness Princess Ethelinde?'

'Yes.'

'Sorry to butt in, but shouldn't that be Her *ex*-Royal Highness? Or actually,' Blotto mused, 'should that be Her Royal ex-Highness . . .? I mean, is it the "Royalness" or the "Highness" that is "ex"? Or indeed both of them? Should we perhaps be referring to "Her ex-Royal ex-Highness" . . .?'

'It does not matter!' cried Bogdan Grittelhoff passionately. 'And so far as I'm concerned, ex-King Sigismund is not an "ex-King", anyway. He is still the rightful monarch of Mitteleuropia. It is the vile usurper Vlatislav who will soon be the "ex-King"!'

'What?' asked Twinks, the roses fading from her cheeks.

But Blotto was not about to have his train of logic derailed. 'Except . . .' he pointed out, 'that if Vlatislav is, as you say, a usurper, he's never actually been a "King", so he can't really be an "ex-King".' Then he added helpfully, 'He could be an "ex-usurper", if you like.'

'We are wasting time,' hissed Bogdan Grittelhoff, 'and what you seem to forget is that I am dying here!'

'Yes. Sorry. Just thought it was an interesting point of protocol.' An idea came to Blotto. 'And now you come to mention it, I suppose you'll soon be an ex-bodyguard. And, if you're actually dying, an ex-person.'

'Never mind that,' said Twinks. 'Bogdan Grittelhoff, you claimed just then to be a supporter of ex-King Sigismund –'

'Of *King* Sigismund, for heaven's sake! I am the loyal one. It is my brother Zoltan who is the traitor!'

'Are you telling us –?'

'I am telling you, milady, the truth.'

'But –'

'And you will hear me out, just as I had the good manners to hear you out!' The effort of this shout seemed to have increased the flow of blood, which had now seeped through his trousers and was pooling on the dusty floor around his feet.

'Would you like us to staunch that?' asked Twinks, rather belatedly. 'I'm sure we could find some towels or table cloths . . . or whatever it is that servants put on wounds.'

'No!' the man replied stoutly. 'A Grittelhoff knows when to die!'

'Oh, that's all right then. If you can manage to get your explanation out before you do . . . well, it would be frightfully convenient . . .'

Bogdan Grittelhoff took a deep, rasping breath. 'It took a long time for me to believe in the duplicity of my brother Zoltan. We were together from the womb.'

Blotto coughed discreetly. 'There's no need for language like that. There is a lady present, and ladies shouldn't know about things like wombs.'

But the dying man ignored him. 'We were twin fruits of the same stem. In everything we were together. We are both, I believe from birth, loyal to the ruling dynasty of Mitteleuropia. It is only in the past few days that I have come to understand the depths of my brother's duplicity.'

'What, while you were at Tawcester Towers?'

'Exactly, milady. Only a few days ago I overhear Zoltan talking to Captain Schtoltz. The Captain has been given a secret mission by King Sigismund. He was to infiltrate the court of the Vlatislav in Zling and to assassinate the usurper. But then I hear that he and my brother have other plans. In fact, Captain Schtoltz was also in the usurper's pay, and the mission on which he was really going back to Mitteleuropia was to find an assassin who will return with him to kill King Sigismund!'

'At Tawcester Towers?' asked Blotto, shocked.

'Yes.'

'But, I mean, getting to Mitteleuropia and back, not to mention finding an assassin . . . well, that's all going to take a week or so . . .'

'Undoubtedly.'

Blotto looked appalled. 'And ex-King Sigismund and his lot were still reckoning to be at Tawcester Towers in a week or so? That long? I mean, there's some proverb thingie about fish and chips or –'

Twinks cut across him. 'So that was why you killed Captain Schtoltz?'

'Of course. To protect the rightful King of Mitteleuropia!'

'And why did you kill Pottinger?'

'Because I overhear him too. In conversation with my brother Zoltan. And they are planning to kidnap Princess Ethelinde!'

90

'So,' said Blotto slowly, 'your dash down here in the Frimmelstopf roadster – nice car by the way, but I'm afraid not a patch on the Lagonda – was to prevent the ex-Princess being kidnapped by your brother?'

'Of course!' Again the shout weakened him. His breath now came with the creak of leaking bellows. 'And nearly I succeed. Zoltan is here with the girl, waiting for the motor launch which will spirit them away to the Continental shore, and thence to Zling where the girl will be in the clutches of her evil uncle, the vile usurper Vlatislav!'

'Was the ex-Princess –?'

'Milady, she is still the Princess,' he moaned.

'Very well. The Princess . . . was she aware that Zoltan meant her no good? Because apparently she left Tawcester Towers with him willingly.'

'By the time I arrived to save her, she had worked out for herself that my brother was up to no good.'

'Erm, you say,' Blotto ventured, '"by the time I arrived to save her", but, erm . . . well, looking round, it doesn't look as if you succeeded in saving her.'

'No. There is no end to my brother Zoltan's treachery. I tell him the only way to settle our dispute is to fight a duel. That is the Mitteleuropian way when there is a dispute between brothers . . . as I am sure it is the way in all civilized countries.'

'Well, no, actually,' said Blotto, 'quite often here the two boddos'll each get another ten boddos together . . .'

'And have a pitched battle, yes?'

'No, have a game of cricket, actually. Amazing how cricket takes away all the . . .' He struggled for the right expression.

'Will to live?' suggested Bogdan Grittelhoff.

'No, no. Annie Something . . .?'

'Animosity?'

'That's the fellow, Twinks. Thanks. Anyway, after a good game of cricket . . . Were you actually there that night when I explained the rules over dinner, because if you weren't, I could happily give you a quick –'

91

'I don't think the gentleman has time for the rules of cricket,' said Twinks softly. She looked across at the spreading pool of blood. 'Or much else, come to that.'

'Oh. Right.'

'So, Mr Grittelhoff, I gather you fought a duel for the Princess and lost?'

'I did not lose, milady! Unless it is losing to be shot by your opponent before you have even turned and started pacing away.'

'That is not losing. It is bad luck.'

'And it wouldn't happen in cricket,' Blotto pointed out, 'because in cricket there are rules for . . .'

The rest of his sentence was quenched by a look from his sister. For a moment the only sounds in the room were the rattling gasp from Bogdan Grittelhoff's throat and the soft dripping of his blood on to the floor. Then Twinks spoke again. 'So the important question is – where are your brother Zoltan and the ex-Princess Ethelinde now?'

With a supernatural effort of will, Bogdan Grittelhoff rose to his feet and pointed out of the hut's cobweb-shrouded window. His hand stretched outwards in a gesture of futile heroism, as he cried, 'There!'

As they rushed to the window, Blotto and Twinks heard the thump of his body hitting the floor. They didn't really have time to think that, as last words, 'There!' hardly won the coconut. Very unlikely to make it into a Dictionary of Quotations.

There was just enough light over the harbour for them to see dark-suited sailors cast the motor launch off from its moorings. They heard the roar of its powerful engines as the boat sped contemptuously away from the south coast.

And they saw, pathetically outlined against the stern rail, the forlorn figure of Her Royal Highness ex-Princess Ethelinde.

Or possibly, thought Blotto, Her ex-Royal ex-Highness ex-Princess Ethelinde.

12

The Family Honour

'The fact is, Blotto,' said the Dowager Duchess, 'that we have to do something about it.'

'Yes, Mater.' Her son sounded subdued, as though he were still at school and had just been accused of roasting a smaller boy over his study fire.

'Or rather,' she went on, '*you* have to do something about it. The family honour is at stake. I know he's only an ex-King, but if it gets round the courts of Europe that guests are not safe at Tawcester Towers ... well, what kind of a reputation will the Dukes of Tawcester have? And obviously Loofah can't do anything ...'

Blotto agreed there. Loofah could never do anything. Except be Duke, and that didn't take much doing. When it came to adventures, the younger brother was the family specialist. Though from what his mother said next, Blotto realized that wasn't her reasoning.

'... because we can't risk the succession by him doing something potentially fatal. No, Loofah's job is to stay here and concentrate on getting Sloggo pregnant with a boy. He can't be gallivanting off on potentially fatal missions to Mitteleuropia. So it'll have to be you.'

Blotto wasn't offended by this. The Dowager Duchess was of the class that was never sentimental about children. And none of them would have questioned that the loss of a younger son was a small price to pay for the preservation of the family honour.

'I'm happy to do it, Mater. In fact, it'll be a privilege. Because I do in a way feel responsible for what happened to the poor girl.'

'Oh no, that's nonsense. Once you start feeling responsible for the intricacies of what goes on in a place like Mitteleuropia . . . well, you'll end up as daft as Rupert the Unhinged. No, it's the wretched people's own fault, and if only the kidnapper had waited until the ex-King and his entourage had moved on somewhere else . . . we'd never have to think about it again. As it is, though . . .' The Dowager Duchess tapped her stick on the carpet of the Blue Morning Room with considerable aggravation and sighed. '. . . we can't really give them their marching orders now. I mean, it's as if one of Grimshaw's staff had stolen a piece of jewellery from a guest . . .'

Blotto was astonished by the concept. 'Surely that'd never happen?'

'Oh, it has done,' his mother replied airily. 'You'd be amazed the horrible things the lower classes get up to. And when something like that does happen – you know, a jewellery theft . . . well, it's a point of honour not to allow your guests to leave until their property has been returned to them.'

'And so, in the case of the ex-Princess . . .?'

'Exactly the same rule applies. I've got to put up with ex-King Sigismund and that tedious ex-Queen Klara and the rest of their ghastly entourage until you bring his daughter back safe and sound.'

'Broken biscuits, Mater! I didn't realize the situation was as serious as that.'

'Well, it is. So, Blotto my boy, time is of the essence.'

'I can see that.' He was about to regale his mother with a little quip about fish and . . . but he couldn't remember how it went. Probably just as well, actually. The Dowager Duchess wasn't much of a one for little quips.

'And what if ...?' he posed the question tentatively. 'What if I fail in my mission?'

'You mean you don't bring the wretched girl back?'

'Yes. Will the ex-King and his lot stay here for ever?'

'Oh no, I think in those circumstances, we'd be absolved of any further obligations of hospitality ... provided you had *tried*, of course.'

'Oh, Mater, I would *try*.'

'No, that'd be fine.' A moment of dubiety crossed the Dowager Duchess's craggy features as she searched her memory for ancestral precedents. 'Well, it'd certainly be fine if you tried and failed, *but died in the attempt* ... That'd be absolutely tickey-tockey.'

'Don't worry, Mater, I won't fail.' Blotto knew what belonged to a hero. 'And if I do – *and die in the attempt* – at least I'll die knowing the family honour is intact.'

'Yes. So, Blotto my boy, you'd better start flexing your muscles, buckling on your breastplate, girding your loins and all that kind of stuff. Remember ...' She fixed him with the eye whose demands he had never, from the nursery onwards, been able to refuse. ' ... every moment you delay is another moment I have to try and think of something to say to ex-Queen Klara.'

'I'll be off before the day is out.' He looked out of the mullioned windows at the darkling shadows that crept across the lawns of Tawcester Towers. 'Well, today actually nearly is out, but I'll be off tomorrow morning at worm's first waking yawn.'

'That will be acceptable. Oh, by the way, Blotto, I don't want you travelling alone.'

He looked at his mother with incomprehension. Was this the first recorded instance of the Dowager Duchess actually showing concern for one of her offspring? 'Why's that, Mater?'

'Well, you don't speak any Mitteleuropian, do you?'

'Not a cuckoo-spit.'

'So you'll need an interpreter.'

'Yes . . .' He was confused, searching for something. Then into the innocent fog of his mind came the sudden sunburst of an idea. 'I say, Twinks speaks Mitteleuropian.'

'Are you suggesting your sister should accompany you?'

'Well, it is a notion. And I'm sure she'd love to do it.'

'What she would love to do is neither here nor there. You, Blotto, are about to embark on a very dangerous mission . . .'

'And it's no place for the ladies – is that what you're saying? Because Twinks can be a bit of a girl when it comes to –'

'No. The point is that Twinks is my only daughter. If something happens to her, I don't have another one. Whereas, with you . . . well, there's always Loofah.'

'Yes, take your point, Mater, right.'

'And I'm still hoping to breed from Twinks,' said the Dowager Duchess firmly. 'So who will you take with you to Mitteleuropia, Blotto?'

The answer was instant. 'Corky Froggett.'

'Excellent. That common little chauffeur who used to be in the army. Salt of the earth. Totally invaluable – and completely expendable.'

'Yes. Mind you, Corky doesn't speak Mitteleuropian.'

'As I recall, he hardly speaks English. Anyway, don't worry about that. Ex-King Sigismund is organizing an interpreter for you – and also a cover story.'

'A cover story?'

'Yes. You know what a "cover story" is, Blotto, don't you?'

He brought the full power of his brain to bear on the question. 'Erm . . . is it the bit of the story that's on the outside of a book?'

'No, you nincompoop! In this case, it's the reason why you're going to Mitteleuropia.'

'But I know that. I'm going to Mitteleuropia to rescue ex-Princess Ethelinde.'

'Yes, but you can't tell people that, can you?'

Blotto was shocked. 'Are you saying you want me to lie? Because I was always brought up to believe –'

'Oh, for heaven's sake! Don't worry, ex-King Sigismund will tell you what to say.'

'Very well.'

'He requested that you should go and see him as soon as possible.'

'Yes, of course, Mater.' Blotto rose from his chair and made for the door, but was frozen by the sound of his mother's voice.

'Oh, one thing . . .'

'Yes?'

'Still family honour and all that . . .'

'Mm?'

'If you do rescue ex-Princess Ethelinde . . . there's a very strong chance that you'll be expected to marry her.'

Blotto felt as though he had just been struck over the head with a claw-footed bathtub. 'Why?'

'Well, two unchaperoned young people scampering across Europe together . . . it's hardly the thing, is it?'

'No, but –'

'And traditionally, under such circumstances, the kidnapped girl and her rescuer do tend to fall in love.'

'Yes, but –'

'I think ex-King Sigismund would be very keen on such an alliance. Joining the ruling house of Mitteleuropia to the Tawcester dynasty . . . yes, he'd like that.'

'How do you know?'

'Because we have discussed the matter.'

'Oh.' Blotto felt the freedom that surrounded him being drained away, as by a suction pump. 'But – but – but – but . . .' He sounded like a small car going up a very steep hill.

'Of course,' the Dowager Duchess went on, 'it will depend on whether ex-King Sigismund remains an ex-King or not . . .'

'Oh?'

'Well, I can't have you marrying an *ex*-Princess, can I?'

'No,' Blotto agreed, hope beginning to dawn. 'No, that'd be awful. Going against family history. Rupert the

Stuck-Up would really have disapproved of something like that happening.'

'But, on the other hand, if your mission is successful . . .'

'If I manage to rescue the girl, you mean?'

'Not just that. If you manage to rescue the girl, and bring down the regime of the usurping King Vlatislav, and restore ex-King Sigismund to his rightful throne – which is the kind of thing I'd expect from any son of mine, Blotto . . .'

'Well, obviously I'll do my best.'

'. . . then ex-King Sigismund will be *King* Sigismund . . . and ex-Princess Ethelinde will be *Princess* Ethelinde . . . and there'll be absolutely nothing to stop you from marrying her!'

'Oh, broken biscuits,' murmured Blotto.

He was in something of a bind. Family honour demanded that he should be successful in his quest. But the more successful he was, the more at risk he would be from the threat of marriage to ex-Princess Ethelinde . . . or Princess Ethelinde, as she would then be. Bit of a candle-snuffer, he reflected.

13

A Top Secret Mission

Blotto's interview with ex-King Sigismund took place in the suite above the library which the Mitteleuropian party had commandeered. In fact they met in the room where the unfortunate Captain Schtoltz had choked out his last breath. The covered bed and shrouded furniture suggested that no one else had taken up residency after him. In the middle of the room stood a large object draped in a dust-sheet, whose contours did not fit any piece of furniture that had come within the compass of Blotto's experience.

The usurped monarch was accompanied by the Margrave von Humpenstaupen who, with the escape of one Grittelhoff brother and the demise of the other, seemed to have taken over the role of royal bodyguard. This must have been an onerous task for someone who, up until that point, appeared to have devoted most of his energies to cultivating his moustache.

'I cannot overemphasize,' ex-King Sigismund began, 'the vital importance of the mission you are about to undertake.'

'Don't worry,' said Blotto, 'I'm up to it. I've played cricket. I'll get your daughter back.'

'I am pleased to hear of your confidence, but I think you should be aware of the seriousness of the situation in Mitteleuropia. My usurping brother Vlatislav has ears everywhere.'

'Does he?' asked Blotto, anatomically puzzled until he vaguely remembered something one of the beaks at school had said about metaphors.

'In the remotest village of Mitteleuropia there are spies.'

'Well, that's all right,' said Blotto. 'I'm not going to the remotest village in Mitteleuropia. I'm going to the capital. Should all be tickey-tockey there.'

'I mean, wherever you go in Mitteleuropia, there will be spies.'

'What? Foreign spies?'

'No, Mitteleuropian spies.'

'Well, I'll be snickered . . .' murmured Blotto. 'I mean, our chaps at the War Office sometimes send spies out to other countries . . . nasty business, but has to be done for national security and all that guff . . . but we'd never have any on home ground.'

'In Mitteleuropia Vlatislav has spies everywhere. In Zling every second person is a spy.'

'Broken biscuits . . . Well, this brother of yours does sound a shabby stencher. What, so he's set up a whole system of secret police, has he?'

'No. He has taken over my system of secret police. That is why I know how efficient they are.'

'Oh.'

'There is one thing I must advise you: *in Mitteleuropia trust no one*. Even the people you think to be your friends, they could easily be in the pay of my evil usurping brother Vlatislav. People change allegiances as readily as ladies change hats. There is a Mitteleuropian proverb: *He whom you trust at ten o'clock will stab you at one minute past*. Take nothing at face value. Once again I say: *in Mitteleuropia trust no one*.'

'Get your drift.' Blotto nodded sagely. 'Leave it with me.'

'So, Right Honourable Devereux Lyminster, you have to be very careful who you speak to – and what you say to them.'

Blotto didn't think it was probably the right moment to correct the ex-King on his use of titles. 'Don't worry, Your ex-Majesty –' the expression on the ex-regal face suggested that he too was having problems with foreigners' use of titles – 'I mean Your Majesty. I know how to clam up, like a . . . well, like a clam.'

'It is therefore important that we have a cover story which is foolproof – very important in your case.' Had there been any implied insult in this sentence, Blotto was blithely unaware of it. 'So I will hand over to the Margrave von Humpenstaupen, who will tell you what your cover is.'

'Good ticket. So tell me, Margrave, who am I going to be?'

Von Humpenstaupen ran his fingers through his luxuriant moustaches like a Chinese Emperor assessing a bolt of fine silk. 'What matters is that the persona you take on is believable. Nobody must smell a rot.'

'I think you possibly mean "rat".'

'Rat, yes. King Vlatislav –'

'*Usurping* King Vlatislav,' said ex-King Sigismund testily.

'Of course, Your Majesty. *Usurping* King Vlatislav is a man of much suspicion and he has made all Mitteleuropia deeply suspicious too. Everyone in the country is a septic.'

'Sceptic.'

'Yes. So when suddenly an aristocratic Englishman crosses the Mitteleuropian border at the town of Zbrik, everyone is going to wonder why he is there.'

'And,' said the ex-King, 'it is of paramount importance that no one ever finds out the reason for your journey. If the truth is discovered, it could threaten danger to the person who is dearest to our royal heart.'

'Ah,' said Blotto. 'You mean your ex-daughter?'

This prompted another burst of ex-royal irritation. 'She is not my ex-daughter!'

'Oh no, sorry, right. Get your drift, anyway. I must not reveal to anyone that the real purpose of my mission is to rescue ex-Princess Eth – I mean, Princess Ethelinde?'

'Exactly. Whatever pressures are put on you.'

'I'll be as silent as a butler's shoes.'

'Even under torture?'

'Even under torture.' As he repeated the ex-King's

words, a question rose naturally to Blotto's lips. 'Why, are they likely to use torture?'

'Very likely. I trained my secret police well. If torture were an Olympic sport, the gold, silver and bronze medals would all be won by Mitteleuropians.'

'Oh, congratulations,' said Blotto. 'So we need a good cover story for me ...'

'I have already devised –'

'I say,' said Blotto, so excited by his idea that he forgot his manners and interrupted. 'Couldn't I have gone for the hunting? You said the hunting's pretty beezer in your country.'

'Yes. But you could not hunt in Mitteleuropia without having been invited to hunt there, and since nobody there knows you, nobody is going to issue you with an invitation, are they?'

'No. Rodents to that idea then.'

'What we need,' said the Margrave von Humpenstaupen, 'is something that will make you welcome in the country, and will automatically give you a way in to all the top bras.'

'Top brass, I think.'

'Top brass, right. So, in other words, you have to go to Mitteleuropia taking with you something that the Mitteleuropians want, something they lack.'

'Oh, hoopee-doopee!' An idea irradiated Blotto's perfect features. 'I could offer to teach them how to play cricket!'

The expression on the two Mitteleuropian faces suggested they didn't share his high opinion of this solution. Nor did they buy his supporting argument that a knowledge of cricket couldn't fail to turn the usurping Vlatislav into a decent bloke with a proper understanding of right and wrong, who would immediately hand the kingdom back to his brother and spend the rest of his life in the nets, blamelessly trying to improve his cover drive. Blotto was disappointed by their reaction, because he rarely had ideas of quite such dazzling quality.

The Margrave von Humpenstaupen did not even bother to vocalize his reaction, but continued as if the suggestion

102

had never been raised. 'What we must concentrate on is the personality of the *Usurping* King Vlatislav.' No danger of him making the same mistake twice. 'He is an evil, vicious man, in whose heart there is no room for potty.'

'Pity, I think.'

'Yes, pity. He is a tyrant, and how do tyrants impose their wills on their people?'

'Sorry, you've got me there,' said Blotto. 'Haven't met that many tyrants . . . well, except for Mater, of course.'

'Tyrants impose their will by causing pain, by hurting people. Wherever there is a tyrant, there will also be violins.'

'Violence, perhaps?'

'Violence, yes. So . . . what we have to use to attract the *Usurping* King Vlatislav to you is something that he needs to continue his course of viol . . . *ence.*'

'How do you mean exactly?'

'I mean this.' With a dramatic gesture, the Margrave von Humpenstaupen swept away the dust-sheet to reveal the mysterious object in the middle of the room. It was a machine gun, gleaming with evil intent.

'The Accrington-Murphy,' said the Margrave von Humpenstaupen. 'The latest model, capable of greater and speedier destruction than any weapon yet invented. The *Usurping* King Vlatislav would kill to get one of these.'

'And then kill a lot more when he'd got one, eh?'

'Exactly. If he had this, he would be as happy as a clamp.'

'Clam.'

'Clam, yes.'

'So you're suggesting I should zap off instantly to Mitteleuropia and present him with this as a rich gift?'

'No, no. If you did so, he would be instantly suspicious. He would small a rut.'

'Rat.'

'Damnation, yes. I knew it wasn't "rot", but I got the wrong bowel.'

'Vowel.'

'Yes. What I am suggesting is that you should go to Mitteleuropia and offer to sell him Accrington-Murphys. This is a sample only. If he knows you have access to these machines, *Usurping* King Vlatislav will be very keen to place an order for many more.'

'Yes,' ex-King Sigismund agreed, suddenly animated. 'So that he can visit even more cruelty upon *my* people.'

'Just a minute,' said Blotto. 'Are you suggesting that I should act as a *gun-runner*?'

'Why not?'

'Well, is it the kind of thing that a member of the British aristocracy should do?'

'It is the kind of thing for which many members of the British aristocracy were granted their titles.'

'Oh well, that's all right then,' said Blotto. 'So I won't have to change my name? No spoffing funny noses or false moustaches?'

'No, the fact that you are who you are will ensure your welcome at the court of the *Usurping* King Vlatislav.'

'Good ticket.' Blotto was relieved. Remembering his own identity had always been a bit of a struggle. Remembering somebody else's might just be too much of a challenge.

'Besides,' the Margrave von Humpenstaupen went on, smoothing out any residual wrinkles in the Englishman's conscience, 'you will not actually be being a gun-runner. You will only be *pretending* to be a gun-runner.'

'Oh, right, that'll be absolutely beezer.' Blotto cast a dubious eye on the machine gun. 'If I'm going to be pushing this spoffing contraption to the Usurping King, I'm going to have to know how it works, aren't I?'

'Have no anxiety,' the Margrave replied. 'Its operation is extremely simple. You point it at your enemies, press this button here and – poof – they are lying on the ground bleeding.'

'Oh, maybe I should have a go.' Blotto moved towards the gun with enthusiasm.

'I think not. Depending of course on how much you value the furniture and fittings in this elegant room.'

'Oh, get your drift. Yes, Mater might get a bit frosty if I smashed this place up.'

'Besides,' said the ex-King, 'you do not need to worry about the mechanics of the weapon. Your chauffeur Corky Froggett is fully up to date on its operation.'

'He would be.' Blotto grinned. 'Anything that involves killing people, Corky's your boddo. All right, I'll pretend to be a gun-runner for you.'

'Excellent. It is the perfect cover story,' ex-King Sigismund enthused. 'It is guaranteed to appeal to my vile brother. You will gain access to the innermost circles of his court at Zling.'

'Oh, good. I hope he speaks English.'

'Very little. I was the brother who spent his childhood at his studies. He was the brother who spent his pulling the wings off insects and small birds.'

'Ah,' said Blotto. 'Now this could be a bit of a chock in the cogwheel. You see, when it comes to passing the time of day with a chap in Mitteleuropian . . . I'm about as much use as a panama hat to an Eskimo.'

'Don't worry,' said the Margrave von Humpenstaupen. 'this too we have thought of. You will not be alone on your trip to Zling.'

'No, I know that. Corky Froggett's coming with me. But if you're expecting him to be the star of the *salons*, splashing around the *bons mots* in Mitteleuropian . . . well, quite frankly . . . A lot of people can't understand his English, let alone –'

'No, I was not talking about your shover.'

'Chauffeur, right.'

The Margrave suddenly rose to his feet, crossed the room, and opened the door. As if he had been waiting for his cue, a slight young man, dressed in subservient black, entered.

'Allow me to introduce your new manservant – who will also act as interpreter for you in Mitteleuropia – Klaus Schiffleich!'

14

Goodbye to Tawcester Towers

Blotto didn't want to cause any demarcation ructions with Grimshaw's staff, so he let his usual manservant Tweedling prepare his clothes for packing. Klaus Schiffleich would take over his duties once they were on the road.

His garments were neatly laid out in the dressing room for him to check through. This was merely a courtesy. Someone of Blotto's class never looked to see what had been packed for him. If on his travels something was found to be missing, he simply saw to it that Grimshaw sacked the manservant responsible.

But that evening there was one thing extra that he wanted packed – and packing it was a task he was prepared to undertake for himself. Although the suggestion had been summarily rejected by the ex-King and the Margrave von Humpenstaupen, Blotto still thought his idea for taming the combative nature of the Mitteleuropians was a good one.

Reverently, he reached into the bottom of a cupboard and extracted his cricket bat. That block of English willow had served him well, and bore its scars like a proud warrior. In spite of the loving and frequent libations of linseed oil with which it had been anointed, the surface was dented with the red marks of sixes past, the abrasions of googlies countered and yorkers parried. Blotto wasn't much of a one for sentiment – didn't do for boddos to be soppy – but the sight of his bat always stirred strong inarticulate sensations within his chest. The bat carried his memories – not only the great ones, like his unbeaten century in the Eton and Harrow match, but also of lesser moments. Every sweep and hook and drive of his cricketing career was etched into that noble wood. The bat was his life. He cared about it more than words could say. Blotto couldn't ever imagine feeling the same kind of emotion for a woman.

He placed it in the bottom of one of his valises. In the unpredictable world of Mitteleuropia he'd feel more secure knowing that he had his cricket bat with him.

Blotto, Corky Froggett and Klaus Schiffleich were going to make an early start in the Lagonda the following morning. Tickets had been arranged for the ten o'clock ferry from Dover to Calais. So Blotto, who never had trouble sleeping but who needed his full nine hours, planned an early night.

Before he turned in, though, he wanted to have a bit of a chinwag with his sister. Twinks was such a brainbox, he was sure she'd have a lot of good advice on what he should do in Mitteleuropia. He still felt a little disappointed that she wouldn't be coming with him, though he fully accepted the Dowager Duchess's point that Twinks shouldn't be put at risk while there was still a chance of breeding from her. With Loofah's efforts in that direction still drawing blanks (or rather girls, which came to the same thing) a male heir from some marriage contracted by their sister might yet – with a bit of jiggery-pokery from the lawyers – secure the family line.

Though Blotto did not lack bravery – indeed he had always had a propensity to run blindly towards danger – he knew that, when it came to devious planning, he was a prize cauliflower. And he suspected that the rescue of ex-Princess Ethelinde from her usurping captors might be a job that required some devious planning. Which being the case, he was going to need a bit of a steer from his sister.

Twinks's brilliant mind was always full of beezer schemes. The secret extradition of a kidnap victim would be exactly her size of pyjamas, and she would undoubtedly be able to tell him the best way to achieve it.

But, bizarrely, as he searched round Tawcester Towers that evening, there was no sign of Twinks. The Dowager Duchess hadn't seen her. Nor had Grimshaw or any of his network of staff. Her personal maid had no idea where she might be, but did not think it could be far away as she had not been given instructions to pack anything and all her mistress's clothes were in place in their wardrobes.

Blotto was mildly frustrated at not being able to have his consultation with Twinks, but he wasn't about to send out a search party for her. His sister, he knew, was her own woman. He also knew – though he tried to pretend he didn't – that a lot of the chaps found Twinks dashed attractive. Though he could never imagine her to be anything other than chaste, he knew as well that some men were rotten stenchers, who might try to arrange clandestine encounters with an unchaperoned Twinks. This was not an area of her life that had ever been discussed in conversation between them, and Blotto was very happy that that arrangement should continue. Basically he reckoned that, if his sister was indulging in some kind of private life, then it wasn't his place to probe.

So he reconciled himself to not seeing Twinks until his return from Mitteleuropia, went to bed and sank into his customary untroubled sleep of the innocent.

15

Foreign Climes

Blotto had never really seen the point of travelling. He had nothing against foreigners or foreign countries – awfully nice places and awfully nice boddos, he felt sure – but he had everything he needed in England. In the past there had been trips with school chums to shuffle off wodges of spondulicks in the casinos of Paris and the French Riviera, which had all been quite jolly, but he'd never felt less than relief to get his feet back on home soil. Life became so much simpler when a chap was surrounded by people who spoke the King's English.

Still, he had no prejudices – or no more prejudices than anyone else of his background and education – and approached the forthcoming trip to Mitteleuropia with a mixture of curiosity and excitement, tempered of course by the understanding that he was upholding the family's honour. And also the knowledge that, the sooner he could get back with ex-Princess Ethelinde, the sooner his mother's duty of hospitality to the ex-King and his entourage would cease. Tawcester Towers would once again be the exclusive domain of its rightful owners. Fish and guests and all that . . .

Still, he was setting out on an adventure, and if there was one thing that appealed to the Right Honourable Devereux Lyminster, it was an adventure. Going to foreign climes for recreation might be pointless, but going for an adventure was a different ticket altogether.

It might have been thought that three men crossing Europe with a machine gun in the dicky of their Lagonda would attract the attention of border guards and Customs officers. But at a mere flash of Blotto's British passport and the sight of his name all curiosity from such hirelings evaporated. Since the Middle Ages the bloodlines of the Dukes of Tawcester had intertwined incestuously with most of the royal houses of Europe, and even a younger son was still afforded appropriate deference by lackeys at national borders. One curious official at the Belgian frontier did ask the passengers what the blanket-wrapped object in the dicky was, but on being told it was an 'Accrington-Murphy', lost further interest.

Conversation in the Lagonda bubbled along pleasantly enough. Blotto and Corky Froggett had been through so much together that there was never a lack of stuff to talk about. As they entered each new country Corky would reminisce fondly about how many of its nationals he had killed in battle, and Blotto would bemoan their lack of cricketing expertise.

Klaus Schiffleich took a lesser part in the dialogue. For a start, he was a manservant, so obviously a certain distance had to be maintained. Also he was Mitteleuropian, which automatically diminished the conversational topics which he and his new master might share. But he was a benign, if slightly effete, presence in the Lagonda, and did contribute the occasional observation in his high-pitched, almost girlish, voice.

And as a manservant he couldn't be faulted. In fact Tweedling could have learnt a thing or two from Klaus Schiffleich. In the various hostelries at which the party stayed overnight, he slept dutifully on the landing in front of his master's door, as a deterrent to larcenous landlords. And in the mornings hot water, clean linen and edible breakfasts were scrupulously procured. Blotto, who as a rule didn't much notice domestics, found nothing in the young man's services to complain about. And he knew that, once inside Mitteleuropia, when translation services would be required, Klaus Schiffleich would really come into his own.

The only detail about his new manservant that offended his master was the fact that he wore perfume. Blotto had already expressed his opinion on that subject when the cologne of the Grittelhoff brothers had been discussed. There had to be something dashed peculiar about a chap who was offended by his own manly odour. Maybe something in a Mitteleuropian upbringing encouraged such namby-pamby self-indulgence. If they'd played cricket, you wouldn't catch their young men wandering round like mobile tarts' boudoirs. But clearly, in that matter, Klaus Schiffleich was a lost cause.

What made the situation even more incongruous was the fact that the perfume he wore was very reminiscent of one that Blotto's sister Twinks favoured.

The manservant, however, did demonstrate his worth in other ways. It was he for instance who, as they approached the Mitteleuropian border, noticed the fact that they were being followed.

'See the black car behind us,' he said in his accented falsetto. 'It has been tailing us all the way from Baden Gaden.'

'What make is it?' asked Blotto.

'It's a Klig. Vehicle of choice for the Mitteleuropian secret police.'

'Do you want me to lose them, boss?' asked Corky Froggett, revving up the Lagonda's powerful engine in anticipation of a cross-country dash.

'I'm not sure. What do you think, Schiffleich?'

'They're not doing us any harm,' the young man replied. 'And their presence suggests that the cable we sent from the telegraph office in Kuckowspitz got through.'

'True,' said Blotto. They had contacted the Mitteleuropian Ministry of the Interior to announce their imminent arrival in the country. And also revealed that they were carrying a prototype Accrington-Murphy with them.

'I wouldn't worry about the surveillance,' Klaus Schiff-leich squeaked on. 'They're just letting us know they're aware of our presence.'

'And would that be common practice in your country?'

'Oh yes, in Mitteleuropia the spies of the Usurping King Vlatislav are everywhere.'

'So you don't think the boddos in the car behind mean us any harm?'

'I don't think so. But, if they do, we'll find out as soon as we reach the Mitteleuropian border post. If we get any trouble there, then we may have to fight our way out of it.'

'For which very reason,' Corky Froggett announced sonorously, 'I have brought *these* with me.' He opened the Lagonda's glove compartment to reveal three highly polished automatic pistols.

Blotto was dismayed. 'Oh, I didn't think we were going to use guns.'

'I think we may need to, milord,' said his chauffeur.

'But I hate using a gun. It's the coward's weapon. If there's a scrap looming, I'd much rather just ask the other boddo to put up his dukes and thrash the thing out, man to man, according to the old Marquess of Queensberry's rules.'

'I'm afraid, sir, that the Mitteleuropians are as ignorant of the Marquess of Queensberry's rules as they are of the laws of cricket.'

'Poor old thimbles. What kind of a life is that?' Blotto was deeply moved. 'And bad luck, Schiffleich. You must have had a really rotten time growing up in Mitteleuropia.'

'I survived.'

'Yes, but it can't have been much more than survival . . . with no cricket . . . or boxing . . . and without even speaking English . . .'

Corky Froggett decided it was time to halt this spiral down into the maudlin. 'Anyway, given the fact that the Mitteleuropians don't abide by the Marquess of Queensberry rules, I think you should each have one of these.' He handed across two of the guns and stuffed the third into the pocket of his black uniform.

'For emergency use only,' said Blotto firmly. 'Just in case there's any rodentry at the border.'

But there wasn't any. Though there were a large number of armed guards at the crossing, dressed in dark green uniforms with tall black helmets and looking capable of any atrocity, no weapon was raised against the new arrivals. The party in the Lagonda were not only expected, but also welcomed. It was the magic of the Accrington-Murphy that saw them through. Like all illegal regimes, the government of the Usurping King Vlatislav needed firepower to enforce its evil schemes.

So, after the briefest exchange of courtesies and a waving-away of the proffered passports, the Lagonda was ushered into the Kingdom of Mitteleuropia. The fact that the black Klig was a government-sanctioned escort was confirmed when it was allowed through the checkpoint without even stopping. The huge car continued to follow some three hundred yards behind the Lagonda.

Blotto's first sight of Mitteleuropia was an impressive one. It was at times like these, encountering scenes of such beauty, that he wished he was more articulate. When he returned to Tawcester Towers all he would be able to tell his mother by way of description was that there were 'lots of trees and mountains'. But that was a poor representation of the way the crenellations of almost black pine trees climbed steeply up from the roadway until they petered out where the Mitteleuropian Alps showed snow-covered tips like the peaks of over-whipped cream.

In spite of its great beauty, there was something unsettling about the landscape. Late afternoon when they arrived, they got the impression that the sun had never irradiated the dark slopes that pressed down on them. Nature here did not seem benign, rather it was a malevolent force, forever encroaching, strangling the life from everything that lay in its path. Even Blotto, who wouldn't have recognized the atmosphere of a place if it had jumped

up and kicked him in the throat, could sense that Mitteleuropia was vaguely sinister.

There were many bumpy side roads which spiralled off
to get lost in the darkening woods, but the main thorough-
fare to Zling was straight and well surfaced. They saw
very few other vehicles on the way to the capital, and those
they did were all horse-drawn. The only other motorized
transport was the shadowing Klig behind them. As the forest thinned and the landscape flattened, small fields and
primitive thatched huts were visible at the sides of the
road. Blotto had his prejudice confirmed that Mitteleuropia
was still a peasant economy, some fifty years behind the
British Isles in all aspects of development.

And when they could see their destination, Zling, spread
out before them, it looked much more like a medieval than
a modern city. The conurbation was built around a small
hill, that stood out like a boil on the smooth skin of the
plateau. On top of this promontory was a large slate-grey
castle.

Blotto pointed it out to Klaus Schiffleich and asked, 'Is
that the Berkenthingywhatsit that the ex-King kept going
on about?'

'No,' the young manservant replied. 'Berkenziepenkatzenschloss is situated some fifty miles from Zling. What
you see before you is the Korpzenschloss, traditional family seat of the Schtiffkohlers since the thirteenth century
when King Sigismund the Bald defeated the Turks at the
Battle of Glitsch.'

'Oh, right, and is that where we'll find King Vlatislav?'

'Usurping King Vlatislav, yes.'

'Oh yes, of course, must get his title right.'

'Though,' Klaus Schiffleich hastened to say, 'I think it'd
be better if, to his face, you did call him "King Vlatislav".'

'Good ticket,' Blotto responded. 'No, I suppose he's not
that keen on the old "Usurping" label. Leave it with me.
All be tickey-tockey, don't you worry. You can rely on
me to –'

What Blotto could be relied on to do was never revealed,

114

because at that moment Corky Froggett slammed on the Lagonda's brakes. From a side turning on the outskirts of Zling, a vehicle had suddenly swung out in front of them.

'What's up? Is this a kidnap attempt?' demanded Blotto.

'No,' replied Klaus Schiffleich. 'Just the second part of our escort. See, it's another Klig.'

And so it proved. The car in front of them was identical to the one behind, which had now taken closer order. With only a car's length space either end, the Lagonda allowed itself to be led through the medieval stone gateway of Zling and over cobbled streets towards the Korpzenschloss. In the fading evening light there were few citizens on the streets of the capital. Those who were there, hooded frightened figures wrapped up in cloaks, showed little interest in the gleaming Lagonda or its contents. As soon as the convoy of cars approached, they scuttled away up side alleys like crabs disturbed in a rock pool.

The nearer they approached, the huger the Korpzenschloss loomed over them. It didn't have the comforting chunkiness of an English castle; instead it rose in a profusion of ever taller towers, looking like an outgrowth of some exotic – and undoubtedly poisonous – fungus.

All the approaches to the main gates were heavily sentried by soldiers with antiquated rifles and fixed bayonets. They wore the same dark green uniforms and black pointed helmets as the border guards. At apertures in the stone frontage of the castle the evening light caught the gleam on the barrels of machine guns (much less sophisticated models than the Accrington-Murphy). The soldiers' looks were ugly, but again the presence of the two Kligs front and back of the Lagonda ensured that the new arrivals were not challenged.

The escorting cars left no doubt as to where the Lagonda should stop, directly in front of the Korpzenschloss's main gates.

'Right,' said Blotto. 'Time for you to show us the colour of your Mitteleuropian, Schiffleich. If anyone starts spouting at me, I won't understand a spoffing word.'

115

But he needn't have worried. As soon as he stepped out of the Lagonda, Blotto heard the English words, 'Welcome to Mitteleuropia, the Right Honourable Devereux Lyminster.'

And he found himself facing King Vlatislav. Or, to be strictly accurate, the Usurping King Vlatislav. But he wasn't about to say that to the chap's face.

16

Dinner with the Usurper

Dinner in the Korpzenschloss was a splendid affair, though it included too many courses and sauces for Blotto's taste. He favoured meals where large slabs of meat were served with the simplest and unfussiest of vegetables. Sauces always made him suspicious. Like flowers at a funeral, he felt there must be something unpleasant they were trying to hide.

But the Great Hall of the castle, in which the dinner was served, was an impressive sight, its walls hung with weaponry and coats of arms, its vaulted ceilings trailing the colours of vanquished foes. One complete wall was given over to portraits of the Kings of Mitteleuropia. They were, to Blotto's eyes, a shifty bunch, the sort you wouldn't leave alone in a room with your sister's honour. The final portrait was smaller than the pale square of panelling in the middle of which it hung. Clearly, like his throne, the place of King Sigismund's likeness had been usurped by one of his brother.

As is often the case with portraiture, the painted image was more prepossessing than the reality which sat beside Blotto. The Usurping King Vlatislav was, like his usurped brother Sigismund, short and dark. Though his black eyes were wells of deviousness, he did, however, ladle on the charm like a distemper brush dripping with honey. And, in spite of what his brother had said of his abilities, his English was remarkably good.

The usurper also demonstrated some level of gentility in his conversation. Although the only thing about Blotto that interested him was the Englishman's access to Accrington-Murphy machine guns, he did open their discussion to other topics. He asked, for instance, in which way his own position as King of Mitteleuropia differed from that of the King of England.

Blotto didn't know where to start. To mention the two monarchies in the same breath was a travesty of all that was sacred. England was England, whereas Mitteleuropia ... well, that anyone imagined there could be any comparison between the two was preposterous.

But Blotto had been well brought up and he knew that members of foreign royal families were sometimes unaware of their ultimate irrelevance in the scheme of things. As a result, he found himself explaining the British system of government to the Usurping King Vlatislav.

'All right, you've got the King at the top ...'

'And he has power to do whatever he wishes, as I do here in Mitteleuropia?'

'Well, not exactly, no. You see, there's also this bunch of chappies called the House of Commons ... which is actually rather well named ... because a lot of the boddos in there are rather common. You know, some of them didn't even go to *minor* public schools. Anyway, they do all the boring guff ... you know, making laws and increasing taxes and all that. But then there's the House of Lords, which is where our sort of people go, and they do important things ... like seeing that their own particular bits of the countryside get looked after ... and finding ways of avoiding all these taxes that the little oiks in the House of Commons keep raising. It all seems to work rather well.'

'And so your King, what does your King do?'

'Oh, not a lot, really. Well, he does the right sort of things ... the Season, hunting, what-have-you ... And he entertains members of his family ... you know, foreign Kings and Princes ... when they come to visit. Nothing to do with the government, though. He doesn't do any work. He's one of us.'

'And what do you call this system you have?'

'Constitutional monarchy, I suppose.'

'And what does this mean in practice?'

'It means the monarch's nominally in charge, but he doesn't have any power.'

The brow of the Usurping King of Mitteleuropia darkened. 'I do not like the sound of this.'

'Another description of the system is democracy,' said Blotto.

The Usurping King's brow grew even darker. 'This I do not like either. I have heard of it. Democracy means asking the common people what they think, does it not?'

'Well, in a way. You ask, yes, but you don't have to take any notice of what they say.'

The Usurping King's disquiet was still not assuaged. 'Surely democracy is a system of government based on consultation with the common people?'

'No,' Blotto reassured him. 'It's a system based on *the illusion* of consultation with the common people.'

'Ah.' Relief flooded the usurping royal visage. 'So it is not so different from what we do here then. Except that we don't even have the illusion of consulting the common people. And we torture and kill a lot of them.'

'Well,' said Blotto, as ever the last person to condemn another human being or indeed another system of government, 'horses for courses.'

Of course no Mitteleuropian dinner could be complete without the dreaded Splintz. The only advantage Blotto could see of experiencing the ceremony in Zling rather than at Tawcester Towers was that, except for the word '*Zugbash*', he couldn't understand any of the elaborate toasts that accompanied drinking the muck. The Usurping King Vlatislav apologized for the fact that they were spoken in Mitteleuropian – and offered to summon an interpreter, but Blotto said he was fine. No need to drag

119

Klaus Schiffleich out of the servants' quarters, where he'd been billeted with Corky Froggett. 'The feeling of goodwill in the toasts will come across, in whatever language they are couched,' Blotto asserted diplomatically.

'Goodwill?' the Usurping King Vlatislav echoed sceptically. 'There is little goodwill in the toasts we are raising tonight. All of them wish confusion and lingering deaths to our enemies.'

'Ah. Oh. Er, well, good ticket,' said Blotto.

'In particular, confusion and a lingering death to my brother Sigismund, who has had the audacity to lay claim to the throne that is rightfully mine.'

'Has he?' asked Blotto ingenuously. 'Toad-in-the-hole . . . Families, eh?'

A new shrewdness came into the usurper's shifty eyes. 'I wonder if you have met my brother . . .?'

'Oh, I don't think so.' Then Blotto added something that he thought was rather clever. 'This is, after all, my first time in Mitteleuropia.'

'It is not there that you might have met him.' The glare from the dark eyes threatened to peel away a few layers of Blotto's skin. 'I happen to know that my evil brother is currently enjoying the hospitality of Tawcester Towers.'

'Really?'

'Which is the seat of your family, the Right Honourable Devereux Lyminster.'

'Oh, right, yes. I do spend a certain amount of time there.'

'Which means you must have met my brother Sigismund.'

'Not necessarily.' Blotto eased a finger round the inside of his collar which had suddenly become unaccountably tight. 'Big place, Tawcester Towers. Easy to miss the odd ex-King and his entourage.'

'I am sure it is,' said Vlatislav silkily.

But Blotto got the impression he had not really been believed. Time to move the conversation on to a slightly less gluey topic. 'Still, I'm sure you'll want to take a close look at the Accrington-Murphy I've brought with me.'

'Yes, indeed. Tomorrow morning we will have a demonstration of the machine's capabilities.'

'Hoopee-doopee! My chauffeur Corky Froggett will happily put the thing through its paces for you. Where do you want to do it?'

'There is a large square behind us here at Korpzenschloss, which is known as the Square of the Butcher.'

'Why, is there a butcher's shop there?' asked Blotto.

All he got by way of reply was a satirical grimace. 'I think you are having fun with me, the Right Honourable Devereux Lyminster.'

'No, I'm not,' said Blotto, puzzled.

'Anyway, the Square of the Butcher has often been used for such events.'

'What events? Other demonstrations?'

'Demonstrations, yes.' The Usurping King Vlatislav let out a small evil laugh. 'And reprisals for those who take part in demonstrations.'

'Ah. Right. Well, sounds tickey-tockey to me.'

'I will organize some prisoners to be ready tomorrow morning.'

'Oh, we won't need many.'

'Do not worry. I have many. The many deep dungeons of Korpzenschloss are overflowing with prisoners.'

The mention of dungeons reminded Blotto – almost for the first time since he left England – of his true mission in Mitteleuropia. He had been sent to rescue ex-Princess Ethelinde. Maybe she, even as he spoke, was directly beneath him, languishing in one of Korpzenschloss's dungeons.

But of course he didn't mention that thought as he clarified his meaning. 'What I meant was that we wouldn't need many because the Accrington-Murphy's not very heavy. One of its big selling points. We won't actually need any prisoners. Corky Froggett'll be able to carry it on his own.'

'It is not for carrying duties that I will be organizing the prisoners.'

'Oh, for what then?'

'It is for target duties I will be organizing them.'

Blotto looked bewildered. Then, like a shy spring crocus, understanding blossomed. 'Target duties? You mean you're going to use these prisoner johnnies as something to shoot *at*?'

'Exactly. If your Accrington-Murphy does not shoot anyone, I will not know how well it works, will I? Come on, you would not buy a horse without having taken it for a ride, would you?'

'No,' Blotto agreed uneasily.

'In exactly the same way, you would not buy a machine for killing people until you have actually seen it killing people.'

'But who are these prisoner johnnies? I mean what have they done?'

The Usurping King's eyes flashed danger as he replied, 'They have dared to question the right of my claim to the throne of Mitteleuropia.'

'Oh, get your drift.'

'And death is the sentence imposed on anyone who dares to question that right.'

'Broken biscuits,' murmured Blotto.

At this moment their conversation was interrupted by the appearance at the Usurping King's side of a weasel-faced man in a black uniform with silver frogging. Blotto wasn't aware of the man actually arriving. One moment he wasn't there, the next moment he just was.

Vlatislav apologized to his guest and then let the newcomer whisper in his ear. Even if Blotto had heard what was said, he would have been none the wiser, because the man spoke in Mitteleuropian.

At the end of the message, the Usurping King nodded approval and the man was reabsorbed into the shadows at the edge of the Great Hall. 'This is good news,' Vlatislav announced.

'Oh, tickey-tockey,' said Blotto. 'Something you can share with me?'

'Let it just be said that another of my enemies has been captured.'

Blotto couldn't think of anything better to say than another 'Oh, tickey-tockey.'

'He too is now in the dungeons of Korpzenschloss.'

'Oh, tickey-tockey,' said Blotto for the third time. Conversational originality had never been his strongest suit.

'And he, I think, would be a very suitable candidate to attend tomorrow morning's demonstration of your Accrington-Murphy.'

'You mean he'll be shot?'

'If your machine gun is as efficent as it is meant to be, yes.'

'Oh.' Something didn't feel quite right to Blotto. 'But will he have had a trial?'

'By the morning he will have confessed to his evil plotting.'

'How can you be so sure?'

'I am sure. Everybody in the dungeons of Korpzenschloss confesses eventually. In most cases very quickly. And some,' the usurper continued with some pride, 'are still alive after they've confessed.'

'I think maybe our legal system is a bit different,' Blotto suggested tentatively. 'We in England have this kind of judicial practice called "Trial by Jury".'

'And we in Mitteleuropia have many kinds of our own judicial practices. For instance –' the Usurping King Vlatislav grinned with glee – 'tomorrow you will witness "Trial by Accrington-Murphy".'

'And how exactly does that work?' asked Blotto, not sure that he wanted to know the answer.

'It is very simple. If the bullets from the Accrington-Murphy pierce the skin of the prisoner, we know him to be guilty. If he is unharmed by them, then he is innocent. So he has what you in England I think call ... "A Sporting Chance".'

The Usurping King beamed and then burst into a long, fruity laugh. He seemed to find the whole business a lot funnier than Blotto did.

17

A Traitor Revealed

Blotto's mouth felt as though it had been scoured with wire wool by an over-assiduous scullery maid. Splintz really didn't agree with him. He reckoned by the time the average Mitteleuropian died, he must have a completely hollow body, all internal organs having been eroded by constant intake of the noxious fluid.

Still, at least the evening was over, and he had finally been allowed to escape to the privacy of his room. Outside the door stood two green-uniformed, black-helmeted guardsmen, armed with fixed-bayonet rifles. If they were there to give the guest to Korpzenschloss a sense of security, they failed in their mission. Blotto had the distinct feeling the guards were there to prevent him from leaving the room rather than to protect him against intruders.

The bedroom was decorated in the style of a family mausoleum, with tall barred windows which couldn't have provided much illumination even in daylight. High-funnelled oil lamps shed a flickering light over the scene. But the large canopied bed looked comfortable, and after his long drive – not to mention excessive doses of Splintz – Blotto looked forward to a good night's sleep. His dressing gown and pyjamas, he noted approvingly, were laid out on the bed, and Klaus Schiffleich stood in an appropriate posture of deference at the side of the room.

'Is there anything else you require, milord?' asked the manservant. Once again his master was struck by the high pitch of the voice. Almost as though it hadn't broken yet. Maybe, he concluded, like everything else in a backward country like Mitteleuropia, puberty arrived late.

'Tell you what would really fit the pigeon-hole,' replied Blotto. 'An octuple brandy and soda. I know, as a Mitteleuropian you may have been virtually weaned off your mother's breast on to the stuff, but I'm afraid, as far as I'm concerned, the only proper use for that Splintz of yours would be removing barnacles from a boat's bottom. I need something to wash the taste off my tonsils.'

'I have anticipated your request,' said Klaus Schiffleich. 'You will see there is an octuple brandy and soda already standing on your bedside table.'

'Oh, good ticket. Just give me a minute to gird the old loins in jim-jams and I'll be wallowing in the B and S like a dying man at an oasis.'

As the young man helped him out of his evening wear, Blotto found the pistol that Corky Froggett had given him. 'You still got your one of these, Schiffleich?'

'Yes, milord.'

'Better give it to me for safe-keeping.'

'But why, milord?'

'Not good form, servants carrying guns, don't you know? Kind of thing that could cause ructions below stairs.'

'Well, if you're sure . . .'

'I am sure. Hand it over, Schiffleich.' The manservant did as he was told and Blotto stowed the two pistols in the bottom of one of his valises. As he was doing so, he saw his faithful cricket bat and gave it a sentimental pat and a stroke.

While the young man helped him to change into his nightwear, Blotto observed, 'Must be a bit of a homecoming for you, Schiffleich. Zling born and bred, are you?'

'In a manner of speaking, milord.'

'Hm.' Blotto felt his nostrils once again invaded by a not-unfamilar perfume. A perfume that would have sat

125

perfectly on his sister Twinks, but wasn't really quite the thing when splashed all over a manservant. 'Tell me, Schiffleich . . .'

'Milord?'

'Are you wearing cologne?'

'Yes, milord.'

'Well, could you kindly desist from doing so in future? The British Empire wasn't built by namby-pambies going round smelling like spoffing florist's shops.'

'No, milord. Mind you, I would like to point out that, as a Mitteleuropian, building the British Empire is not high on my list of priorities.'

'Maybe not, but you are on my side. We're on this mission to protect the honour of the Tawcester family, and the interests of the Tawcesters and the British Empire have always been identical. So no more of the spoffing cologne tomorrow – right?'

'Very good, milord.'

Successfully installed into his pyjamas, Blotto made for the brandy and soda. 'So tell me, Schiffleich, where have they billeted you in this rabbit warren?'

The young man indicated a small door behind him. 'There is a small anteroom there, milord, with just a truckle bed in it. I will be there, sir, all night, to protect you if necessary.'

Blotto laughed at the suggestion. The idea that he could be protected by Klaus Schiffleich was incongruous. Putting aside false modesty, Blotto knew himself to be a well-proportioned slab of solid muscle at the peak of physical fitness. Whereas the young manservant was so slight – hardly larger in figure than dear old Twinks – and the innocence expressed in his azure eyes, pale skin and ash-blond hair did not suggest he would be a match for the feeblest of assailants.

Still, didn't do to point out a chap's deficiencies – even when that chap was only a servant. 'I'll sleep all the better, Schiffleich, knowing you're there,' said Blotto magnanimously. 'And I think sleep's probably what I need right now.

126

Good for the old brain, sleep. I always hope I'll wake up with a more efficient brain than the one I went to sleep with.' He may have always hoped for that, but sadly it never happened. 'Because tomorrow I've really got to work out how I'm going to rescue ex-Princess Ethelinde.'

'That is the aim of your mission here, certainly, milord.'

'Yes. I'm sort of going on the assumption at the moment that the poor little thimble is being held against her will somewhere in this very castle.'

'That's entirely possible, milord. Korpzenschloss is renowned throughout Mitteleuropia for the extent of its dungeons. There is a positive labyrinth of them, carved into the solid rock of Zling. That would be the obvious place to start looking for the ex-Princess.'

'Good ticket, Schiffleich.' For a moment Blotto looked wistful. 'Must say, I feel a bit alone on this mission . . .'

'But why, milord? You have me here to assist you – not to mention the bloodthirsty Corky Froggett.'

'Yes, but . . .'

'What is it, milord?'

'Fact is, Schiffleich, I've got a sister called Twinks. That's not actually her proper name, but that's what I call her. And when it comes to investigation and all that sort of rombooley she's the absolute lark's larynx. If old Twinks were here, she'd know exactly how to snuffle out the ex-Princess. Trouble is, though, Twinks isn't here.'

'Are you sure?'

'Of course I'm sure, Schiffleich. She's hundreds of miles away.'

'She might be nearer than you think.'

Blotto looked at his manservant in amazement. Klaus Schiffleich had spoken the last sentence in almost perfect English. No trace of an accent. Proper upper-class English, the very kind that Blotto and Twinks had been brought up to speak.

'There, Schiffleich! You can speak English. You don't need that spoffing Mitteleuropian accent, do you? Well, why on earth didn't you start speaking properly before?'

'Can't you guess?' came the reply, again in perfectly modulated English.

'No, I can't. And I'm afraid, Schiffleich, it's too late for me to start playing guessing games with servants. What I need is some shut-eye. Before that, though, what's required is . . . a quick baptism in this magnificent B and S.'

But as he raised the glass to his lips, Blotto stopped, with the shocked expression of a man whose filling had just dropped out. The repeated admonition of ex-King Sigismund rose to the surface of his mind. *In Mitteleuropia trust no one.* And he remembered the native proverb he had been told: *He whom you trust at ten o'clock will stab you at one minute past.*

Blotto looked suspiciously at his Mitteleuropian manservant. 'Did you prepare this brandy and soda yourself, Schiffleich?'

'That was not possible, milord. The bottles of alcohol and other catering supplies we brought in the Lagonda were impounded on our arrival here at Korpzenschloss.'

'I see. So where did you get the drink from?'

'I asked one of the guards outside the door to order it from the castle's butler.'

'In that case –' Blotto handed the glass across – 'I would like you to drink some of it before I do, Schiffleich.'

'Well, if you really want me to, Blotto . . .'

As the manservant took the glass and a hefty swig, his master bridled. Blotto had always prided himself on his common touch, but there were limits. And when a servant used the first name of a titled gentleman to his face, such a limit had been breached.

'I'll thank you, Schiffleich, to call me "milord".'

'Oh, don't be so stuffy, Blotto me old gumdrop.' This, from a servant, was even more offensive. And copying his accent in that way was positively insolent, thought Blotto as the young man went on, 'Can't you see that I'm –?'

But who it was that he claimed to be was not at that moment to be revealed. Klaus Schiffleich swayed suddenly, reaching an effeminate hand up to his temple. His azure eyes glazed, as he fell to the ground, unconscious.

Blotto knew he had had a narrow escape. Ex-King Sigismund had been right. *In Mitteleuropia trust no one.* Even the King's own appointee, Klaus Schiffleich, was now revealed to be a traitor. The young man had organized the brandy and soda to knock out – or possibly even kill – his new master.

Blotto opened the door of his room. In the corridor the two green-uniformed guards eyed him suspiciously from beneath their black helmets.

'There is a criminal in my room,' said Blotto. 'He is currently unconscious, which should render your task of removing him very easy. See to it that he is incarcerated in one of your deepest dungeons.'

The magnificence with which he made this speech was rather diminished by the fact that neither guard understood a word of it. Eventually, Blotto had to resort to sign language to demonstrate to them what had happened. But when he used the word 'prison' they got his meaning. Unceremoniously picking up the limp body of Klaus Schiffleich, they removed the traitor from the room and summoned other guards to arrange his imprisonment.

One up to me, thought Blotto proudly. I have foiled the first evil plot against my safety here in Zling. I have removed the first viper from my . . . well, from whatever part of a boddo's anatomy it is where vipers go.

And as he settled down in his canopied bed to sleep the sleep of the just, Blotto's last thought was: Twinks would be really proud of me.

18

Crying in the Night

There were always two dominant instincts within the noble breast of the Right Honourable Devereux Lyminster. One was his love of chivalry, the other was his love of sleep. So when he was woken up later that night by the sound of a woman's crying, Blotto got as near as he ever did to a moral dilemma. Half of him knew he ought to be leaping on to a metaphorical white charger to alleviate the damsel's distress. The other half desired only to turn over in his sumptuous Mitteleuropian bed and continue his interrupted slumbers.

It was a tough choice and, had not the feminine weeping suddenly increased in volume and urgency, he might well have slept on through till the morning. As it was, honour demanded that he take some action. Struggling reluctantly from the horizontal to the vertical, Blotto belted his dressing gown about himself, stepped into his monogrammed slippers and out on to the landing.

The first thing he observed was the absence of surveillance. Of the two guards whom he had last seen manhandling the perfidious Klaus Schiffleich off to prison there was now no sign at all. The dimly lit corridor was ominously empty and silent ... but for the increasingly loud weeping which, Blotto could now identify, issued from the bedroom next to his own.

He approached the door and made a tentative tap on its

dark surface. This prompted only another surge of hysteria from within. He tapped again more loudly, but still receiving no words of permission to enter, took it upon himself to open the door.

The room was probably about the same size as his own, but the light from the single oil lamp by the bedside did not penetrate its furthest extremities. The outlines of what lay on the bed were also blurred by the draperies of translucent scarlet silk that descended from the canopy above, but Blotto could still recognize that it was a woman. From whom the crying continued to emanate.

'Um . . .' he began, but then realized his usual conversational gambit might not be adequate to the current situation. He tried an 'Erm, well . . .' instead, and went on, 'What's up, old thing? Hit a sticky patch, have you?' he asked, assuming that the weeping woman understood English. 'Man trouble, is it?' he added, vaguely remembering that his sister had once said this was an affliction that affects the supposedly weaker sex.

At the sound of his voice, the red hangings were thrust aside, and he found himself looking at someone wearing less than any woman he'd ever encountered. (Which, in Blotto's case, was actually not saying a lot. Given his upbringing, the only areas of female flesh he had ever seen were faces and hands.)

The woman wore what he would have described as 'a golden kind of strapping sort of thing which covered the sticky-out bits of her upper body' and golden trousers which were slashed to show a lot of what Blotto could only assume were legs. (He always had his suspicions that women had legs rather in the same way that men did, but this was his first visual proof of the fact.) Between the 'strapping thing' and the trousers was an area of uncovered dusky midriff.

Blotto boggled. He stared at the woman mesmerized. At that moment, you could have snaffled major organs from his abdomen and he wouldn't have noticed.

'Erm, well . . .' he said again. 'Sorry, we haven't been introduced. I'm Devereux Lyminster, but everyone calls me "Blotto".'

Wiping her eyes with one hand, she extended the other for him to kiss. Blotto shook it.

'And I . . .' she said in a voice as thick and opaque as frozen honey, 'am Svetlana Lubachev.'

For once she told the truth. That was her real name. Blotto, having never stirred far from Tawcester Towers, had not heard it before. If he had done, he would have been aware of what he was dealing with, and been on his guard against her feminine wiles.

Because Svetlana Lubachev had the most developed feminine wiles of anyone in the twentieth century. Or the nineteenth. Or any century, come to that. She was just about the wiliest female ever. Though still technically married to a Polish count, whose bride she had become as a rather mature fifteen-year-old, since then her list of lovers had encompassed most of Europe's royal families. (There was indeed a scurrilous rumour that it was her ambition to have had a lover from *all* of Europe's royal families. And that she was only two short of her target.)

Many men had tried to describe her, but their accounts of her beauty differ. They all start with the eyes, dark as chocolate sauce, and then seem to become vague about her other charms. A magnificent décolletage is mentioned by many, but that's about it. The hypnotic powers of her eyes seemed to have stripped her paramours of all descriptive skill. (She slummed once by having an affair with an untitled, though internationally renowned, poet, and even he didn't get much further than saying that she was 'jolly pretty', and writing a poem in which 'love' rhymed with 'the stars above'.) But, if the precise details were vague, it was generally agreed that she could have any man she wanted. And that she had had most of them.

Svetlana Lubachev was equally skilled in the arts of the boudoir and the cabinet room. At least three royal divorces had been attributed directly to her influence, along with a couple of depositions and a minor revolution in the Caucasus. She knew the intimate secrets of crowned heads, colonels and cabinet ministers, and it was often she who dictated where the bodies should be buried. And when they were, she remembered the exact locations.

Svetlana was beautiful, devious and ruthless. She used sex like a machine gun. She had cut a swathe through monarchs and left walking wounded in all the palaces of Europe. The man who could resist her wiles had not yet been created.

So, despite their difference in size, when it came to deviousness, to put Blotto up against Svetlana Lubachev was like fixing a match between an angora kitten and an anaconda. (The match-fixer, in this case, had been Usurping King Vlatislav, another of Svetlana's lovers, who had entrusted to his mistress the task of ascertaining the real purpose of Blotto's visit to Zling.)

'Well, look, my old bloater, what's your prob?' asked Blotto, trying without marked success to avoid looking at any exposed flesh.

'Oh,' said Svetlana Lubachev, carefully controlling the flow of tears so that they sparkled on her eyelashes but did not threaten to get her make-up streaky. 'Where shall I begin with the problems of a poor feeble woman like myself? They are so terrible, you do not wish to hear them.'

'Oh, all right then,' said Blotto, relieved at being let off the hook.

'But hear them you must!'

'Ah. Well, you don't have to tell me all of them. Just one or two will probably fit the pigeon-hole.'

'Very well . . . what did you say your name was?'

'Blotto.'

'Very well, Blotto. Have you ever had a friend?'

'Oh yes, quite a few. Boddos I was at school with, that sort of thing. People I've met hunting.'

'Have you ever had a really close friend?'

Blotto cleared his throat with some embarrassment. 'Well, no. Chaps don't have really close friends. That is, normal chaps don't.'

'But it is possible for women to have really close friends.'

'Yes, so I've heard. My sister Twinks has got a few chums like that. No holds barred in the sort of things they'll talk about when they get together. You name it . . . hat styles, shoes, even the length of skirts. There's no stopping them.'

'I too have such a friend,' said Svetlana Lubachev tragically. 'I should say I *had* such a friend. Because of her current whereabouts I have no idea at all.'

'Really? Done a bunk, has she? Maybe eloped with some johnnie her parents didn't think matched the wallpaper. Happens quite a lot, I gather . . . at least if the Sunday papers are anything to go by.'

'No, no, my friend would not do anything like that. She knows what kind of behaviour belongs to a Princess.'

Blotto caught on very quickly to that. 'Oh, so she's a Princess, is she?'

'Yes, but a Princess who has suffered terribly, and who dares not put a foot down on the soil of her native country.'

Blotto looked shocked. 'Are you telling me the poor girl's got gout?' he asked.

'No, she is physically well. But for how much longer who can say – given the sufferings that she has to undergo.'

'I think it might clear the fug a bit if you were to tell me your friend's name.'

Svetlana Lubachev breathed the words like a long sigh. 'Princess Ethelinde.'

Blotto's countenance cleared instantly. 'Oh, don't you worry about her. She's all tickey-tockey.'

'Is she?'

'Yes. She was kidnapped in England . . .'

'Was she?'

'Yes, by some bounder called Grittelhoff. And I'm actually pretty sure she's being held in the dungeons of this very castle.'

134

'Then, if, as I say, she is my close friend, why should I not be worried?'

'Because, my old biscuit barrel . . . I am here to rescue Princess Ethelinde. That is the sole purpose of my mission.'

Svetlana Lubachev was frankly disappointed. As a *femme fatale*, she did have some standards – not to mention a high opinion of her own abilities. When Usurping King Vlatislav had charged her with finding out Blotto's real purpose in travelling to Mitteleuropia, she had anticipated a long teasing game of cat and mouse. She had relished the prospect of slowly winkling out the truth from the buttoned-up Englishman, of deploying the full arsenal of her feminine wiles, and ultimately perhaps resorting to torture (in whose practice she was at least as skilled as the Mitteleuropian secret police).

But as it was . . . she'd just asked him the straight question and he'd given her a straight answer. She could now report back to Vlatislav, who could arrest Blotto as an undesirable alien and let him join the other prisoners who the next morning were going to prove the efficacy of the Accrington-Murphy in the Square of the Butcher. Really, working with someone like the Right Honourable Devereux Lyminster just took away the fun from the whole business of *femme fatalisme*.

Still, Svetlana Lubachev had a task to complete. Vlatislav wanted more than a confession from Blotto; he wanted the young man actually to be caught in the act of trying to rescue the Princess. It was up to Svetlana to organize that. She'd already arranged the absence of the two guards on the corridor. Now all she had to do was to send Blotto down towards the dungeons, where he would be intercepted as he was breaking into Princess Ethelinde's cell.

Svetlana Lubachev reached into what Blotto thought of as her 'golden kind of strapping sort of thing which covered the sticky-out bits of her upper body', announcing, 'I have something in here.'

He didn't doubt it, and couldn't help watching with fascination as she pulled on a golden chain to extract a heavy ring of keys from her capacious bosom. How something so substantial had been concealed there prompted new conjectures in Blotto's mind about the precise details of female anatomy.

'These,' Svetlana breathed on, 'are copies of the keys to all the dungeons of Korpzenschloss. If you can use them to rescue my dear close friend Princess Ethelinde, I shall be eternally in your debt.'

'Don't worry, old pineapple. It's something I was going to do anyway.'

'Why are you, as an Englishman, so concerned with the Princess's safety?'

Blotto was about to say that it was the only way of getting her spoffing father and entourage out of Tawcester Towers, when it occurred to him that that might not be the most chivalrous of responses. So he contented himself with, 'Just one of those family honour things, you know.'

'I understand completely,' said Svetlana Lubachev. She looked at an ormolu clock on the distant mantelpiece, which showed the time to be just after 3 a.m. 'You must wait for an hour before you do anything,' she murmured. 'At four o'clock the shift of the dungeon guards changes. It is precisely then that you must make your rescue.'

'How do I actually get down to the dungeons?'

'At the end of the corridor if you turn left out of my door, you will find a small door studded with metal. There is a spiral staircase there which goes down through eleven floors of Korpzenschloss until it opens into the chamber of the dungeons. It will take you nine and three-quarter minutes to get down there.'

'Excellent.' Blotto stifled a yawn and looked at his watch. 'Right, not for nearly an hour. How am I going to fill that hour? I don't want to risk falling asleep again.'

136

Svetlana Lubachev reached out a hand for his and drew him towards her on the bed. 'First,' she said, 'you have to undo the chain that is attached to the keys.'

'Yes, fine.' So close to her flesh, Blotto felt himself enveloped in the intoxicating miasma of her perfume. 'Is it one of those little jiggly hook things?'

'Yes,' sighed Svetlana, as his hands clumsily tried to work the fastening open. 'Are you a married man, Mr Blotto?'

'Good Lord, no. Don't need any of that guff. Life's full enough with hunting and cricket.'

She chuckled. 'So you are unattached?'

'I'm currently attached to this spoffing great chain. Whoever fixed this round your neck certainly didn't mean it to come off in a hurry.' As he concentrated on the clasp, his face was so close to Svetlana's that he could feel her warm breath on his skin.

'Blotto,' she exhaled, 'you are a very attractive man.'

'Oh, don't talk such toffee. I'm no different from the next chap.'

'I would say you are, Blotto. I find you very attractive.'

'Well, you want to get your eyes tested, old thing. Ah,' he sighed with relief as the golden chain came free. 'There – all tickey-tockey.'

He tried to back away, but couldn't. The woman was still holding the end of the chain and seemed to be pulling his face nearer hers.

Svetlana Lubachev had had affairs with all the predictable minor English royals, who, as lovers, she had found totally inadequate. But maybe the country's aristocrats might prove to be more skilled . . .? The Right Honourable Devereux Lyminster was certainly good-looking enough to qualify for her attention. Maybe he might turn out to have hidden skills of the carnal variety. Svetlana thought she might indulge in a controlled sexual experiment.

'Blotto,' she sussurated, 'given the fact that you still have three-quarters of an hour before you can fulfil your mission . . .'

'Yes ...?'

Her voice was as soft as the perfect landing of a hand-tied fly over the mouth of a gaping trout, as she went on, '... would you like to share my bed?'

'That's frightfully decent of you,' said Blotto, 'but they have actually sorted me out with one of my own.'

19

The Secret Prisoner

Blotto was aware that the mission on which he was embarked was a hazardous one. But when he searched the valise in his bedroom before setting off down to the dungeons of Korpzenschloss, it was not the two pistols that he was looking for. He left them in the bag, snugly side by side, as, reverently, he picked up his cricket bat. As he ran his hand down its battered surface and sniffed the evocative smell of linseed oil, he felt suddenly secure. Devereux Lyminster of the house of Tawcester, armed with his cricket bat, would be equal to any foe.

The studded door was at the end of the corridor as Svetlana Lubachev had predicted, and Blotto started his descent of the spiral staircase that led down to the Korpzenschloss dungeons. He didn't count the steps, but there must have been many hundreds, and he reached the lowest level feeling like an overwound elastic band. The slightest jolt, he felt, would make him go 'ping' and unravel at great speed.

The staircase had been dimly lit by irregularly spaced sconces, and there wasn't much more illumination in the chamber at the bottom. It was a wretched space, which Macbeth's witches would have rejected as too dingy for a coven meeting. In the flickering light the green slime of ages glimmered on the encroaching walls, whose only decorations were rusting manacles and other instruments of torture. The ancient doors to the cells were of solid iron,

139

their peepholes closed with heavy shutters. On a dilapidated table bottles, drinking vessels and a couple of sabres suggested recent occupancy, but there was no sign of any guards.

Blotto didn't stop to question this oddity – stopping to question things was not in his nature. All he knew was that he had to rescue ex-Princess Ethelinde as soon as possible. He moved to the nearest cell door and riffled through the ring of keys that Svetlana had given him.

The third one fitted. With a groan like an asthmatic octogenarian being impaled on a toasting fork, the door gave inward. Cricket bat raised as if ready for a bouncer, Blotto advanced into the gloom.

There was silence in the fetid interior, and yet he knew there was someone there. Blotto held his breath, assuming that the cell's other inhabitant was doing the same. See who could hold it the longer.

They both broke the silence with a simultaneous whoosh of air. The whoosh that didn't come from Blotto was accompanied by a rattling of chains.

'Is that you, Princess Ethelinde? I'm sorry, I mean ex-Princess Ethelinde?'

'No!' cried a heavily accented but youthful voice. 'I am not Princess Ethelinde, but I am the man who loves Princess Ethelinde!'

Well, there's a coincidence, thought Blotto. I come in here looking for the ex-Princess, and by pure coincidence I bump into a chap who's in love with her.

But the young man in chains had not finished his burst of rhetoric. 'And I will kill anyone who allows his lips to sully the name of Princess Ethelinde.'

'Who'd want to do that?' asked Blotto.

'You! You have just sullied her name with your lips.'

. 'Oh, I think that's going a bit far. I did mention her name, yes, not arguing about that, but I wouldn't have said I *sullied* it.'

'Anyone unworthy who mentions the Princess's name is sullying it!'

'Ah, well, here, old chap, we get into the question of who's unworthy or not. And I would like to point out that in England, where I come from, I am generally to be reckoned a fairly worthy sort of pineapple.'

'You are from England?'

'Yes. Where on earth did you think I was from?'

'I thought you were from here in Zling. I thought you were another of Usurping King Vlatislav's evil guards who had come to give me a beating with that club.'

'This isn't a club.'

'Then what is it?'

'It's a cricket bat.'

'Oh.' The young man's attitude changed instantly. 'Do you mean to say that you play cricket?'

'Yes.'

'Then I'm frightfully sorry that I even suggested that you might be unworthy, or indeed that you might sully Princess Ethelinde's name. The lips of a man who plays cricket could never sully anything.'

'That's jolly decent of you to say so. I take it, by the way, from what you're saying, that you play cricket too?'

'I have played a little. I am trying to introduce the game into my country.'

Blotto was ecstatic. 'Here? You're trying to introduce cricket here? Hoopee-doopee, I knew there was bound to be some cricket somewhere in Mitteleuropia!'

'Mitteleuropia is not my country.'

'Oh. Perhaps it's time for a few introductions? I'm Devereux Lyminster, younger brother of the Duke of Tawcester, but everyone calls me "Blotto".'

'I think I have heard of you – or possibly read about you in Wisden. Are not you the very Right Honourable Devereux Lyminster, who once scored a hundred and seventy-six in the Eton and Harrow match?'

'Guilty as charged,' said Blotto, with a self-deprecating chuckle.

There was a rattle of chains as the invisible prisoner tried to shake his hand. 'I'm really honoured to meet you.'

'And sorry, you haven't said who you are yet . . .?'

'I am Crown Prince Fritz-Ludwig of Transcarpathia.'

'Ah. And can I ask what you're doing in this dungeon? Presumably not just visiting?'

'No. I have been imprisoned by the vile lackeys of the wicked Usurping King Vlatislav.'

'When?'

'This very day.'

Suddenly something very rare happened. Two thoughts within Blotto's brain connected. 'You must be the johnnie he mentioned at dinner.'

'Sorry?'

'I dined with the Usurping King Vlatislav this evening. And in the course of the meal a vile lackey came and gave him the news that one of his enemies had been captured.'

'Yes,' Crown Prince Fritz-Ludwig confirmed. 'He would have been referring to me.'

'So what have you done to put a needle up old Vlatislav's nostril?'

'What have I not done? Ever since the vile usurper purloined this country, I have been determined to unseat him from his stolen throne. You see, King Sigismund of Mitteleuropia and his entourage were guests of my father, King Anatol of Transcarpathia . . .'

'Oh yes, he told me that when he was at Tawcester Towers.' By now his eyes had accustomed themselves sufficiently for him to see that Crown Prince Fritz-Ludwig was a blond young man with a gossamer-thin moustache and beard. In the manner of Continental royalty, he wore a uniform so tasselled and frogged with gold that it could have been melted down and made into a substantial dinner service.

'Well, ever since the evil coup –' Blotto refrained from responding with another 'Coo' – he knew it would only lead to complications – 'I have been determined to restore the status quo. It is, you see, a matter of family honour.'

'How come?'

'Ex-King Sigismund and his entourage were guests of

142

the Trancarpathian royal family when his throne was snatched. Until the rightful King is restored to power, our family honour will be sullied.'

Back to sullying, thought Blotto. He was about to say that he was in a similar gluepot, having to settle an issue of family honour before he could get the ex-King and wretched entourage off the premises at Tawcester Towers, but he decided it might not be tactful.

'Anyway,' Crown Prince Fritz-Ludwig of Transcarpathia continued, 'I have been planning a counter-coup. All of the might of the Transcarpathian army are, as we speak, massed a mere five miles away on the border of Mitteleuropia, waiting for the signal to invade.'

'And is ex-King Sigismund – I mean, King Sigismund – aware of your plans?'

'He should be. I sent a special emissary to him at Tawcester Towers to inform him of my intentions.'

'I say,' said Blotto, having another of those rare moments when two thoughts connected. 'Chappie's name wasn't Captain Schtoltz, was it?'

'It was.' So at last there was an explanation for the murder at Tawcester Towers. 'Do you know, Blotto, if he managed to get my message to the King?'

'Can't be sure, but I think he may well have been prevented by a bad tomato called Zoltan Grittelhoff.'

In the pale prison light Crown Prince Fritz-Ludwig's face turned even paler at the sound of the name. 'Zoltan Grittelhoff! I always suspected that he was a traitor! He and his brother were with the King in Bad Vibesz when the coup happened.'

'Right.' Blotto managed to see the face of his watch in the thin light. It was nearly half-past four. 'Maybe we ought to push on the pace pedal? Don't know how long it'll be before the guard johnnies turn up again. Didn't you say something about the Transcarpathian hordes waiting for a signal to invade?'

'Yes. I was on my way to give the signal when I was captured by the vile lackeys of Usurping King Vlatislav. If my forces do not see the signal by five o'clock, they will return to their barracks in Bad Vibesz.'

'Then we'd better shift like a pair of cheetahs in spikes. What is the signal they're waiting for?'

'On the highest point of Korpzenschloss there is a beacon, which must be lit before daylight renders it invisible. As soon as its flame is seen through the darkness, the army of Transcarpathia will fire their cannon to let us know they have received the signal. Then they will mobilize, invade and defeat the ill-prepared and ill-disciplined forces of the Usurping King Vlatislav.'

'Hoopee-doopee!' shouted Blotto. 'I'll grab a flaming torch and have that beacon alight in two shakes of a poodle's pom-pom.' And, with cricket bat upraised, he rushed for the door.

'Um,' the Crown Prince shouted after him, 'do you think you could just set me free first?'

'Oh yes, of course.'

'Strength in numbers, eh? The keys to my manacles are hanging from a hook by the guards' table.'

While he was unlocking the shackles of Fritz-Ludwig, Blotto suddenly remembered the real aim of his mission. He'd been distracted by all the talk of coups and counter-coups. 'Actually,' he said, 'I should release ex-Princess Ethelinde too.'

'Princess Ethelinde?' The Crown Prince was thunder-struck. 'But surely she's in England?'

'No, she was with her father at Tawcester Towers, but she was kidnapped from there by Zoltan Grittelhoff!'

'The bounder! How dare he do that to the woman I love?'

'Well, he did do it, and I have information that she's currently locked up in another of these dungeons.'

'That would make sense. The Usurping King Vlatislav is using her as a hostage to force the hand of King Sigismund, just as he is using me as a hostage to force the hand of my father King Anatol. So you're sure Ethelinde is here?'

'That's what my informant told me.'

'Then we must free her!'

144

'Just what I was thinking, Fritzie-boy.'

Blotto was right – or rather Svetlana Lubachev had been right. In the cell three doors away from the Crown Prince's they found the ex-Princess, pitifully manacled as he had been, and still wearing the by-now-rather-grubby dress in which she had left the shores of England.

It was a matter of moments to free her. As he struggled with the key to her chains, Blotto said, 'Nice coincidence, actually, old girl. The man who loves you is here.'

'I know, Blotto,' she said, instantly putting her unencumbered arms about his neck. 'I knew you'd come and rescue me.'

Blotto was aware of Crown Prince Fritz-Ludwig giving him a rather old-fashioned look. Oh, broken biscuits, he thought.

Still, no time to sort out misapprehensions of a romantic nature. The armies of Transcarpathia had to be alerted. 'Come on, let's get this beacon blazing!'

'There is someone else we should release first,' said ex-Princess Ethelinde.

'Oh, really?'

'Your manservant, Klaus Schiffleich, is incarcerated in the dungeon next to mine.'

'Yes, I am,' said a voice sounding uncannily like that of Twinks. 'Please set me free, Blotto! I'm not really Klaus Schiffleich, I'm Twinks!'

For a moment he was nearly fooled. For a moment he was tempted to unlock the door and remove the prisoner's manacles. The voice sounded so like his sister's.

But Blotto wasn't stupid. The words of ex-King Sigismund returned to him. *In Mitteleuropia trust no one.* The traitorous manservant was an excellent mimic, but Blotto already knew that. He wasn't going to be bamboozled so easily. Grabbing a flaming torch from a sconce with his free hand, Blotto shouted, 'No, we'll leave Schiffleich to rot down here! Right, up to the top of Korpzenschloss we go!'

'I don't think so!' The unmistakable voice of Zoltan Grittelhoff echoed through the murky chamber.

145

20

A Short-Lived Freedom

The murderer of Captain Schtoltz stood at the main entrance, flanked by Usurping King Vlatislav's green-uniformed, black-helmeted guards. All of these had their bayonets fixed and barrels pointing towards the escapees. Logic dictated that a cricket bat wouldn't make much inroad into their ranks before its wielder was mown down.

'And of course I recognize you, the Right Honourable Devereux Lyminster. When I heard that you had come to Zling peddling machine guns, I was prepared to give you the benefit of the doubt. But now it seems that was not your mission. You were here to free the enemies of King Vlatislav.'

'*Usurping* King Vlatislav!' shouted Blotto defiantly. 'The rightful King of Mitteleuropia is still at Tawcester Towers!'

Zoltan Grittelhoff chuckled. 'You do not appear to have learned the lesson of *Realpolitik*. Right, you should know, only exists when it is allied to might. Vlatislav controls the armed forces of Mitteleuropia – for that reason he is the country's *rightful* king.'

'Nonsense! No rightful king would employ traitors in the way that the Usurping King Vlatislav does.'

'Which traitors has he employed?'

'Many!' riposted Blotto. 'You yourself are a traitor!'

'No,' said Zoltan Grittelhoff. 'I have always been faithful to King Vlatislav. I have never been a traitor.'

'Then you were a traitor when you pretended to be faithful to ex-King Sigismund.'

'Ah yes,' the former bodyguard conceded. 'You might have a point there.'

'And you were a traitor to my father when you abducted me,' asserted ex-Princess Ethelinde, eager to throw in another accusation.

'Never mind that. Which traitor was it to whom you referred, the Right Honourable Devereux Lyminster?'

'I referred to the traitor who's still in that dungeon over there. The one who you or another of Vlatislav's vile lackeys infiltrated into my personal circle as a manservant. The traitor who calls himself Klaus Schiffleich, and who does a very passable impression of my sister's voice.'

'Where is this person?' asked Grittelhoff.

'I'm in here!' shouted Klaus Schiffleich from behind the iron door of his dungeon. But he had returned speaking with his Mitteleuropian accent.

'And are you, as the Englishman suggests, a traitor?'

'No. I have always been loyal to the cause of King Vlatislav.'

'See?' said Blotto. 'I told you he was a bounder.'

'Very well.' Zoltan Grittelhoff gave instructions to his phalanx of guards. 'Lock these three in that cell over there! And release the man called Klaus Schiffleich from this cell here!'

The guards did as they were told. Resistance was useless, and they herded Blotto, ex-Princess Ethelinde and Crown Prince Fritz-Ludwig back into the Crown Prince's cell. The heavy door clanged shut so hard that the shutter dropped down to reveal its peephole.

Blotto heard rather than saw the release of his perfidious manservant. Klaus Schiffleich spoke to his rescuers in fluent Mitteleuropian, but, as he left, presumably for the benefit of the three prisoners, shouted in English, 'Now you will discover what happens to the enemies of King Vlatislav! Whereas for me, he will I know reward me richly for what I have done!'

Blotto was going to say something cutting, but then

decided not to bother wasting wit on a stencher like that. Just as Zoltan Grittelhoff stepped forward to slam the shutter and leave them in solid darkness, he did however ask, 'And are we to know what plans the *Usurping* King Vlatislav has for us?'

'Indeed you are,' said a new voice. Through the narrow aperture, Blotto witnessed the appearance of the Usurping King himself. The guardsmen all presented arms at the royal arrival.

'Well done, Grittelhoff,' Vlatislav continued. 'You have caught this supposed arms dealer?'

'Yes, Your Majesty. I found him doing what he really came to Zling to do. He was rescuing ex-Princess Ethelinde and Crown Prince Fritz-Ludwig.'

'Exactly as I expected him to do.' The usurper brought his face close to the grille of the cell. 'Hardly the behaviour of an English gentleman, was it, the Right Honourable Devereux Lyminster? Abusing my hospitality in that way.'

'An English gentleman doesn't deal with traitors. The hospitality you speak of is rightly that of your brother Sigismund.'

'Nonsense! Sigismund is an ineffectual dilettante. I am the one who commands the loyalty of the people of Mitteleuropia.'

'Only because you have threatened them with violence.'

'Maybe I have. And let me tell you, as a system of government it works. You'd be surprised how amenable my people are, when they know the alternative is the kind of fate I am planning for your little party.'

'Since the subject's come up,' said Blotto coolly, 'you may as well say what you had in mind for us.'

'Yes, what an excellent idea. Your anticipation will, in that way, become part of your punishment. Tomorrow morning, in the Square of the Butcher there will be a demonstration of the Accrington-Murphy machine gun, which you so generously provided for –'

'All right, no need to tell me any more. I might have known you wouldn't have been capable of thinking up more than one plan. All I hope is that you manage to find someone who can use the Accrington-Murphy properly. They're tricky little beasts.'

'On that account have no fear, the Right Honourable Devereux Lyminster. Your own chauffeur will be operating the gun.'

'Corky Froggett? No chance. He'd never turn a weapon against his master. It isn't in his nature.'

'I can assure you that it is in his nature now.'

'What do you mean, you vile usurper?'

'Have you never heard of *mesmerism*?'

'No, I don't think I have,' replied Blotto. 'Is it some form of political belief?'

'No, you fool! It is a system that works on the brain, so that it can change the personality of any human being.'

'Not Corky Froggett! Nothing could change Corky Froggett!'

'Don't you believe it.' Vlatislav let out an evil laugh. 'In the morning you will have the proof of the efficacy of mesmerism . . . you will see how it can change the human brain . . . when in the Square of the Butcher Corky Froggett and his Accrington-Murphy *will mow you all down like summer corn*!'

With that parting shot, Usurping King Vlatislav slammed down the shutter on the grille and marched off with Zoltan Grittelhoff and his men.

Blotto turned to his fellow prisoners. He couldn't see them in the blackness, but he knew where they were. 'Bit of a sticky wicket we've got to bat on,' he said. 'Wish they'd tried to use that mesmerwhateveritis on me, rather than poor old Corky.'

'Why?' asked ex-Princess Ethelinde. 'Do you think you'd have been able to resist them better than he would?'

'No, but we might have gained some time.'

'How?'

'In my case,' replied Blotto with estimable self-knowledge, 'it would have taken them quite a while finding the brain, before they even started on the mesmer-whatnot process.'

21

An Unexpected Saviour

'Dying's not such a bad thing,' said Blotto, 'so long as you're dying in a good cause.'

'And what would you regard as a good cause?' asked Crown Prince Fritz-Ludwig.

'Preserving the family honour,' Blotto replied automatically.

'And would you say,' asked ex-Princess Ethelinde softly, 'that losing your life to a mechanical firing squad in the Square of the Butcher tomorrow morning will preserve your family's honour?'

'Oh, yes.' Again the response was instinctive, but as he thought about it, Blotto was aware of a potential drawback. His mission to Mitteleuropia had been to rescue the abducted Princess, and the Dowager Duchess had clearly entertained the possibility that he might die in the attempt. But if that were the outcome, where would it place her obligation as a hostess to ex-King Sigismund, ex-Queen Klara and their obnoxious retinue? Would the Mitteleuropians then have squatters' rights to stay at Tawcester Towers for ever? That ghastly prospect brought Blotto firmly round to the view that if he could in some way avoid being mown down by the Accrington-Murphy the next morning, it would be, generally speaking, a good thing.

Mind you, at that moment escaping their pre-ordained fate didn't look to the prisoners a very likely prospect. And

Crown Prince Fritz-Ludwig was demonstrating that rather maudlin tendency that comes over Continentals in death cells. 'If I perish tomorrow,' he said mournfully, 'it will be with one great regret . . .'

'Me too,' said Blotto, trying to stem the downward flow of the conversation. 'My regret will be that I'd really have liked to have scored a double century at Lords . . . but that looks less likely with every passing minute. Is that the kind of thing you had in mind?'

'No, it is something different,' replied the Crown Prince. 'There is one thing I have always wished to do before I die.'

'Yes, I know,' said ex-Princess Ethelinde tartly. 'And I've told you before that you can't. Even if I did consent to the idea – which, by the way, I'm never going to – I would certainly not wish to do it in a filthy place like this.'

The Crown Prince let out a long deflated sigh of disappointment.

'And what about you, ex-Princess – I mean, er, Princess?' asked Blotto, trying to jolly things along. 'Is there something you'll regret not doing?'

'Not really.'

'Oh, good.'

'Until a few weeks ago my regret would be that I have not met the love of my life . . .'

'Ah,' said Blotto, fearful that the conversation might be sailing into choppy waters.

'But since being at Tawcester Towers –' the ex-Princess swelled operatically to her theme – 'I know who is the right one for me. I may regret that that love cannot attain fulfilment, but at least I can die in the knowledge that I have experienced the love of my life.'

There was a silence, and Blotto rather hoped the topic had gone away, but then the Crown Prince Fritz-Ludwig demanded, 'And you're not talking about me as the love of your life, are you, Ethelinde?'

'No,' she replied defiantly. 'There is only one man for me – and that is Blotto.'

151

Oh, broken biscuits, thought the subject of her adoration. We're in a gluey enough spot down here already, without that kind of complication.

'In that case, the Right Honourable Devereux Lyminster,' announced Crown Prince Fritz-Ludwig boldly, 'I will challenge you to a duel for the love of Ethelinde!'

Blotto heard a swish, which he reckoned must be the trajectory of a glove missing his face in the darkness. 'I really don't think that's necessary,' he said in his best conciliatory tone.

'Why not? Are you not a man of honour?'

'Yes, of course I'm a man of honour.'

'As am I. I represent the honour of the whole kingdom of Transcarpathia. And I can see no other solution. We are both in love with the same woman – we must have a duel!'

'Well, yes, if that were the case, I can see that a duel might fit the pigeon-hole. But there's something wrong with your premise.'

'Oh?' queried the ex-Princess. 'What's wrong with his premise?'

Blotto was about to point out the obvious flaw in the argument – that, though the Crown Prince may well have been in love with Ethelinde, he himself certainly wasn't. But before the words could form on his lips, he was suddenly aware that they might represent a lapse of gallantry on his part. To say to her face that he didn't love the girl could be a breach of the Tawcester family's long-nurtured tradition of chivalry. Oh dear, what a gluepot. He rather wished the night was over and he was being escorted out to the Square of the Butcher. That would be preferable to his current dilemma.

'Well, erm . . .' he prevaricated. 'This isn't really the ideal venue for a duel. The fact is, it's pitch dark, we can't see each other, and we haven't got any weapons.'

'We have our fists,' countered the voice of Crown Prince Fritz-Ludwig.

'Yes. Do you do Queensberry's rules in Transcarpathia?'

'I do Queensberry's rules.'

'How's that?'

'Because part of my education took place at an English public school.'

'Oh, really?' Maybe Fritz-Ludwig wasn't such a bad tomato after all. 'Which one?'

But before the Crown Prince could reveal this important piece of information, they were silenced by a 'Ssh' from ex-Princess Ethelinde. There was a sound audible from the other side of their cell door. A metallic scraping. No, they could identify it more accurately than that – it was the turning of a key in the lock!

They all froze, wondering what new tortures or humiliations the Usurping King Vlatislav was about to visit on them. When the door was flung open, for a moment they could see nothing in the unfamiliar light.

Then they made out, standing in the doorway, the slight figure of Klaus Schiffleich.

'You traitor!' cried Blotto. 'Have you come here to gloat at our misfortune?'

'No, Blotto my old gumdrop, I've come to set you free.'

'Oh, very clever – putting on my sister's voice again. Don't worry, I've seen through that little trick.'

'Blotto, I *am* Twinks!'

'No, you're not. Twinks is back at Tawcester Towers.'

'Look, will this convince you?' Klaus Schiffleich removed his cap to reveal a head of ash-blonde hair spun as fine as the filigree of a spider's web.

'Lady Honoria!' said ex-Princess Ethelinde in amazement.

'Now do you believe who I am, Blotto?'

He felt rather sheepish. Faced with the direct question, he mumbled, 'Yes, I do.' And then he added, to keep his self-esteem moderately intact, but untruthfully, 'I knew it was you all along, Twinks.'

22

A Sticky Wicket

'Right, first thing we must do . . .' said Twinks. Oh, how comforting were those words to Blotto. He realized how much he'd missed his sister since he'd left Tawcester Towers. He hadn't been aware at the time, but he'd been under considerable strain for the past few days, the strain of having to think for himself. It was such a relief to have Twinks back, taking over decision-making and all that rombooley.

'First thing we must do is get Princess Ethelinde out of this castle and into the Lagonda on the way back to England!'

'No, actually, Twinks me old muffin, there's something else we need to do first.'

'But rescuing the Princess was the aim of the mission.'

'I know that, but if we can also achieve the overthrow of Usurping King Vlatislav, then that'd be a pretty good Centre Stalls ticket, wouldn't it?'

'Yes, but how can that be done?'

Quickly, Blotto and Crown Prince Fritz-Ludwig explained about the Transcarpathian troops massing on the Mitteleuropian border, and the need for them to be given the signal to invade.

'You're right,' said Twinks. 'That beacon must be lit as soon as possible! We'll only be secure when we hear the cannons of the Transcarpathians!'

'Leave it to me,' said the Crown Prince nobly. 'My country, my squabble.'

'Won't hear of it,' countered Blotto. 'We're in this together!'

'Very well,' said Fritz-Ludwig. 'And we'll pick up and have the duel when we've got the rightful King back on the throne – that suit you?'

'Yes,' agreed Blotto, determined that by the time the counter-coup had achieved its end, he'd be safely back at Tawcester Towers, away from the clutches of both ex-Princess Ethelinde and her amorous swain.

'Then – to the beacon!' cried the Crown Prince, gathering up one of the guards' sabres from the table. 'You'd better take one too.'

Blotto thought about it. He had been Captain of Fencing at school and even represented England at the sport, but somehow swordplay didn't feel right for the current situation. 'No, thanks. I'll feel happier with this,' he said, hefting the weight of his cricket bat in one hand and snatching a flaming torch from its sconce with the other. 'To the beacon!'

It was a lot harder going up more than eleven flights of spiral staircases than it had been going down. But the two young men were fit and, besides, they knew the urgency of their mission. Their reimprisonment had wasted precious minutes, the dawn could not be far away. And the signal beacon, however well lit, would be invisible to the waiting Transcarpathian forces in daylight. If they couldn't see it, there would be no acknowledging cannonade and no invasion.

At least Blotto was with someone who knew his way round Korpzenschloss. As they panted up the stairs, Crown Prince Fritz-Ludwig explained how in happier times he had been a frequent visitor to the castle and knew every last corridor of its massive interior. He had as a child, he said, played with Princess Ethelinde, and it was then he had felt the first glimmerings of the grand passion that . . . Fortunately, before he could complete this soppy avowal of his love, he ran out of breath.

'Top of this next flight,' he managed to gasp out, 'and we'll be on the battlements! Then it's only a matter of yards to the beacon tower!'

'Hoopee-doopee!' cried Blotto, as the two men burst through a small door on to the highest part of Korpzenschloss.

But as soon as they stepped through, they could see that they were expected. They could see the beacon, a wood and kindling-filled brazier atop a pointed spire, but between them and their goal watery moonlight glinted on the helmets and bayonets of at least twenty of Usurping King Vlatislav's guards. As the two young men came into sight, one of them shouted something in Mitteleuropian.

'That's good,' murmured the Crown Prince to his comrade-in-arms.

'What?'

'He said Vlatislav's orders are that we should be taken alive.'

'Toad-in-the-hole!' said Blotto. 'Come on, let's show them what Englishmen are made of!'

'Erm . . .'

'What? Oh, sorry – let's show them what an Englishman and a Transcarpathian are made of!'

Moonlight shone on the Crown Prince's teeth as he grinned with sheer devilment. 'We have the advantage of them! If they have to take us alive, they can't shoot at us. That means they'll just have to use their bayonets. And a sabre's always been a match for a bayonet!' And he stepped forward, slashing at the guards with his huge blade.

'So's a cricket bat,' said Blotto, as he too advanced into the horde, swinging the willow doughtily.

As he rather supected it might, the bat proved a mightier weapon than the sword. Usurping King Vlatislav's troops were trained to deal with Mitteleuropian sabres, but they had never felt the force of an English leg sweep, pull shot or cover drive.

As a result, within minutes Blotto had carved a route through them towards the beacon tower, while Crown Prince Fritz-Ludwig had been quickly surrounded and disarmed. 'Light the beacon, Blotto!' he cried. 'For the honour of Transcarpathia!'

Blotto was actually doing his doughty deeds for the honour of the British Isles and the Tawcester family, but he didn't think this was the moment to explain all that. Instead, he leaped upwards towards the beacon, cricket bat in one hand, flaming torch in the other.

Before he could bring the fire to the waiting wood, however, there was another shout from the Crown Prince. 'Watch it! They're going to shoot the beacon down with their cannons! They're going to destroy it! They're going to –' But he was gagged before he could say more.

Blotto looked coolly down on Vlsatislav's guards. Above them on the rampart opposite stood four ancient cannons, each one manned by a gunner with a flaming fuse and each one trained on the beacon over his head. It would only require one hit to bring the structure crashing down and for ever deprive the Transcarpathian troops of their mobilization signal.

Blotto had a moment of déjà vu. As he thrust his flaming torch into the dry kindling of the beacon and took up a defensive stance with his bat, he was once again at Lord's for the Eton and Harrow match. On behalf of Harrow, Twonker Mincebait's bowling had cut a swathe like the Black Death through the Eton top order. Blotto – or Lyminster Minor as he was still known in those days, even though Loofah had long ago left school and joined the Coldstream – was placed at a modest number seven and, although he'd impressed as a Colt, he was still reckoned to be a rabbit for the big occasion. Hopes among his fellow players weren't high and, although they sent him off from the pavilion with hearty cries of 'Show him what you're made of!', they were all secretly afraid that that was exactly what he would do. And that Lyminster Minor was made of rather inferior stuff.

Twonker Mincebait was an old adversary of Blotto's. They'd been at the same prep school, before following generations of their academic-talent-free families to Harrow and Eton respectively. Twonker had been a couple of years senior and at prep school Blotto had undergone the indignity of fagging for him. (Strange how the British upper classes, destined to spend all their lives ordering servants about, practise at their private schools by ordering each other about.) As a fag, Blotto had suffered no worse than most of his equals. It wasn't the beatings, gougings and the roastings in front of the fire by Twonker Mincebait that he had minded – those he knew were part of the educational system, and character-building – but he had objected to the fact that on the cricket pitch the older boy sometimes questioned the umpire when he was given out. Whatever the rights and wrongs of a decision, questioning it just wasn't cricket.

But Blotto would never say a word against Twonker's skill as a bowler. In Mincebait's hands the ball took on a life of its own, curving slowly down the pitch as if undecided about its own trajectory. It would find a rough patch of grass on which to land, very nearly far enough from the wicket to qualify as a wide, then do a couple of twiddles, a pirouette and a reverse half-chassis around the bat, before nudging gently against the stumps with just enough power to dislodge the bails. Had it been on ice, a Twonker Mincebait delivery could probably have won a figure-skating championship.

So when at Lord's the young Blotto had faced Twonker, beaming devilishly with the confidence of being on the third leg of a hat-trick, he knew exactly what he was up against. And there was already bad blood between them. That blood was hardly purified by the contemptuous ease with which Blotto had sent Twonker Mincebait's first ball for a massive six that landed somewhere in the middle of Regent's Park. Nor was potential septicaemia averted by the fact that he thereafter monopolized the bowling and carried his bat at the end of the match, having secured the victory with an unbeaten hundred and seventy-six.

Blotto remembered the sheer glee of that innings, and he had a rush of the same feeling as he stood on the battlements of Zling, hopelessly outnumbered and armed only with his trusty cricket bat. This was the life, eh?

The gunner of Usurping King Vlatislav who fired the first cannon had none of Twonker Mincebait's finesse. The ball that came thundering out was dead straight. Only Blotto's head stood between it and the column of the warning beacon.

He remembered his training in the nets, waited till the last minute, then raised his bat to tip the ball high above the beacon for a certain six. (In fact it landed in one of the main shopping thoroughfares of Zling, smashing the window of Number 417, the Bonetti Barbershop, which, as Twinks had established, was the only place to sell the exclusive masculine fragrance, Der Jäger.)

But Blotto couldn't worry about where the first ball went, because there was another delivery on its way from the second cannon. This he flipped neatly round to leg and heard the distant sound of it removing a gargoyle from the façade of St Aloysius' Cathedral.

Hardly was that done before the third cannonball was hissing viciously towards him. This one was targeted at the bottom of the beacon column, round about Blotto's knee level. Perfect. He drew his bat back for a sweet cover drive, which sent the cannonball back the way it had come – with interest. Had Usurping King Vlatislav's gunner learned cricket, Blotto might have been out for a 'caught and bowled'. As it was, the ball caught the Mitteleuropian in the midriff and sent him flying out of sight over the top of the ramparts.

But the attack was not over. Not only had the fourth cannon now been fired, but the first of the gunners had had also time to reload, and Blotto realized his next shot would require great finesse and accuracy. In some strange quirk of memory, the first gunner seemed suddenly to have taken on the features of Twonker Mincebait. This was the shot, this was the one he couldn't miss. Blotto played a classic straight bat to the ball from the fourth cannon, driving it fast and true towards the barrel of the first.

The ball disappeared into the cannon's mouth just at the moment the charge ignited. The exiting cannonball met the entering cannonball with a huge impact which flattened both of them and blocked the barrel. As a result, the whole cannon exploded in a shower of fire and metal, which blew the three remaining cannons and gunners way over the battlements.

Following immediately on the blast, Blotto was aware of a great hissing, crackling and spitting above him, as the beacon blazed into ferocious life. And then he heard the welcome sound of Transcarpathian guns booming from the border. They were acknowledging the signal! The invasion of Mitteleuropia had begun!

Blotto smiled modestly and raised his bat by way of salute. He had played longer innings in his cricketing career, but few that had been so satisfying.

23

Betrayed by a Woman!

The effect of the Transcarpathian guns on the Mitteleuropians was instantaneous. The guards scattered in
disarray, showing no regard for their fellows as they
crammed themselves through the doors that led back into
Korpzenschloss. Within seconds Blotto had the ramparts
to himself.

He then realized that Crown Prince Fritz-Ludwig was
not with him. His comrade-in-arms was in the hands of
the enemy! For a moment, Blotto was all set to rush to the
rescue. But a rare moment of rational thought changed his
mind. The mission that had brought him to Zling was the
rescue of ex-Princess Ethelinde. He wasn't there to get
involved in the local politics between Mitteleuropia and
Transcarpathia. Besides, freeing Crown Prince Fritz-
Ludwig from his captors would inevitably lead to the tiresome business of having a duel with him. No, Blotto's duty
was plain. Meet up with Twinks and Corky Froggett, get
the ex-Princess into the Lagonda and head off out of
Mitteleuropia as soon as possible.

He made for the door through which he and the Crown
Prince had come on to the battlements what felt like an age
. . . but could only have been minutes . . . before. Before he
went inside, he noticed that a pinkish dawn was beginning
to break over the snow-capped mountains of the Mitteleuropian horizon. The beacon had been lit only just in time.

There were sounds of commotion and panic inside Korpzenschloss, but he did not see anyone as he descended the long flights of the spiral staircase, cricket bat still triumphantly in hand. He decided he'd pick up his luggage and then meet up with the rest of his party.

Inside the bedroom he laid his cricket bat reverently at the bottom of his valise and closed it. He was just picking up his other luggage when he heard the door open. In the space stood Svetlana Lubachev. Outlined by the light from the corridor, her skimpy costume seemed to melt away, and Blotto felt as if he was facing a naked woman. His tongue was far too well bred to hang out. But he could feel the pressure of it against his lips.

'Um ...' he said, not reckoning he could improve on his usual opening gambit when faced by a member of the fair sex.

'Blotto,' Svetlana Lubachev breathed breathily, 'you are in danger!'

'Really? I thought I had just dealt with it.'

'No. Usurping King Vlatislav is out to get you. His guards will be here any minute.'

'Oh, broken biscuits,' said Blotto, and reached down to retrieve his cricket bat.

'But I know a way you can escape,' Svetlana purred on.

'I don't want to escape. Not without my sister Twinks and Corky Froggett.' He felt sure there was someone else he should have remembered ... 'Oh yes, and ex-Princess Ethelinde.'

'Come with me! I will take you to where they are!'

Blotto needed no second invitation. Grabbing his cases, he followed the woman out of his bedroom, through a secret door in the panelling of the corridor and down yet another narrow spiral staircase.

'This is very good of you,' he murmured.

'It is the least I can do. I want to do my bit to help the restoration of King Sigismund to his rightful throne.'

'You're a good greengage,' said Blotto. It was one of his highest forms of praise.

162

Bluish light grew, as they entered another subterranean chamber. A heavy iron door stood open. 'Your friends are in there,' whispered Svetlana. 'Off that room is a secret passage which leads down to where your Lagonda is ready.'

'Beezer,' said Blotto. 'Can't thank you enough.'

'No time for thanks! Usurping King Vlatislav's guards are not far behind! Quick, through the door.'

'I'll write you a thank-you letter,' said Blotto, as he followed her instructions.

But the moment he was inside the room, he heard the iron door clang shut behind him. He also heard the scraping of bolts being shot home, accompanied by an evil laugh of triumph from Svetlana Lubachev.

24

The Square of the Butcher

There was no sign of humanity – or even life – in Corky Froggett's eyes. God knew by what devilish means the transformation had been achieved, but as he stood behind the gleaming brass of the Accrington-Murphy, he was now a zombie, deaf to everything but the commands of Usurping King Vlatislav. The chauffeur was what he had always been, just a killing machine. But now mesmerism had ensured that he had a new master.

The Square of the Butcher had been a popular place of execution in Zling since medieval times. A long line of Schtiffkohler monarchs had recognized the political value of combining punishment with popular entertainment and, though few had aspired to the ingenuity of Black Sigismund the Sadist, public executions remained very much a part of the Mitteleuropian social calendar.

They were also occasions that kept up with the latest fashions in terms of the methods used. Stoning and breaking on the wheel were considered by the beau monde of Zling to be crude and medieval. The vogue for hanging, drawing and quartering was long past. Burning at the stake had lost its sparkle. Decapitation and garrotting had also had their day. Even the once-exciting innovation of the firing squad had rather lost its lustre.

But mowing down the condemned with the latest model of Accrington-Murphy machine gun offered everything the

Mitteleuropian crowds could have wished for. Such an execution would be yet another coup for Usurping King Vlatislav, and endear him to his people as a supporter of advanced modern technology.

The Square of the Butcher was a natural amphitheatre, which in the thirteenth century had been embellished with raked stone seating on three sides by King Sigismund the Poet and named 'The Square of Beautiful Thoughts'. He had intended the place as a venue in which his subjects would hear extended readings of his rather ornate and inaccessible work, but not a single stanza was ever spoken there, because that Sigismund had soon been killed and replaced in a coup by his brother Vlatislav the Vindictive. (Mitteleuropian history has always had a tendency to repeat itself.) The usurper quickly changed the usage of the venue and renamed it the Square of the Butcher.

For public executions a large viewing platform was always put up for the current King of Mitteleuropia and his entourage. Normally it was taken down between events, but since Usurping King Vlatislav's seizing of the throne he had had so many old scores to settle that the structure had become a permanent fixture.

News of the day's entertainment had spread overnight through the Zling social grapevine, and every seat in the Square of the Butcher had been filled by nine o'clock, a full hour before the fun was due to begin. At about a quarter to ten, the already extensive military presence had been augmented by a large contingent of the King's personal guards, and a few minutes later the day's victims were led out from the dungeons and chained to four upright stone pillars, which stood in front of a wall heavily pockmarked with the evidence of former firing squads.

The appearance of the traitors was greeted by raucous booing, but Blotto and Twinks, the latter still dressed as Klaus Schiffleich, held their heads high. They knew what belonged to an Englishman and an Englishwoman. Ex-Princess Ethelinde and Crown Prince Fritz-Ludwig also held their heads high. Though they were, respectively,

Mitteleuropian and Transcarpathian, Blotto reckoned their exposure to his own countrymen must have taught them what belonged to an Englishman and an Englishwoman too.

'Sorry, Twinks me old muffin,' Blotto had murmured to his sister, as the chains were locked around him, 'to have got you into this gluepot.'

'Not your pawn ticket, Blotto. I got myself into it.'

'Yes, but the Mater will be cross. She was hoping to breed from you.'

'Oh, toffee to that!' Twinks had said. 'Don't think I'm cut from the right dress pattern to make a mother. Larks like this're much more fun.'

'Hoped you'd see it that way, Twinks me old biscuit barrel.'

The booing from the crowd had changed suddenly to ecstatic cheers as, from the entrance opposite the prisoners, Corky Froggett had appeared carrying the gleaming Accrington-Murphy. He set it up in the middle of the square, equidistant between the royal viewing gallery and the prisoners, its barrel pointed firmly in their direction.

His face remained as implacable as a coffin lid. Blotto thought rather wistfully back to the time when his chauffeur had said that, rather than betray his master, he would allow hot coals to be sprinkled liberally over his extremities, have his finger- and toenails extracted one by one, or suffer red-hot branding irons writing the entire Sanskrit alphabet on the most sensitive parts of his anatomy. Oh well, people change. Must find out more about this mesmerism business, thought Blotto. Though he wasn't sure when he'd have the opportunity.

Exactly as the clock of St Aloysius' struck the hour of ten, Vlatislav himself had led the royal party out on to the viewing platform.

His arrival had been greeted by a shouting from the crowds of 'King Vlatislav! King Vlatislav!' so loud and manic that a casual observer might have thought each individual feared punishment if he or she did not shout their loudest (which of course they did).

166

With a single gesture, Usurping King Vlatislav had modestly stilled the ovation. Svetlana Lubachev stood to one side of him. (His mistress was so much more decorative than Vlatislav's wife, Usurping Queen Gerthilde, that he preferred to have her as a consort for public occasions.) Eyes restlessly scanning the crowd, Zoltan Grittelhoff was stationed behind his monarch. And next to the King was a man unfamiliar to the crowds, but who was also dressed in a uniform whose frontage looked like an over-iced Christmas cake.

Vlatislav's first act was to welcome his loyal subjects. Blotto, because of his limited linguistic skills in Mitteleuropian, had no idea what was being said, but Twinks, Ethelinde and the Crown Prince understood every word.

The usurper then introduced the newcomer to his people. 'I would like you to meet my cousin, Prince Rudolph, who is Colonel-in-Chief of the Armed Forces of Transcarpathia.'

The entire crowd intook their breath at the same moment.

'Yes, my friends, you thought that the Transcarpathians were our enemies, but let me tell you that I – I, your loving and benevolent King Vlatislav – have achieved in one night a feat of international statesmanship that could never even have been attempted by the corrupt and disgraced ex-King Sigismund.'

The crowd knew their cues well enough to break into immediate booing and hissing at the name.

Usurping King Vlatislav raised a hand for silence. 'Last night I personally foiled a cruel plot not only against my royal head – which counts for nothing – but also against the peace and stability of my beloved subjects – which counts for everything!'

The crowd vociferously expressed their appreciation of their ruler's magnanimity until they were once again silenced by his raised hand. 'The conspirators behind this plot were the four miscreants you see chained before you!'

He halted the dutiful booing prompted by the revelation and went on, 'I think I'll get through this quicker if you don't react to everything I say. At the end of the narrative I'll raise my hands and you can give me a big burst of applause then.' The crowd was appropriately silent. 'Last night Transcarpathian troops were massed on our borders to invade and help restore to our throne the evil and corrupt ex-King Sigismund!'

A few of the crowd couldn't help reacting with boos to this, but they were quickly shushed up by their neighbours.

'But now, after discussions with my cousin Prince Rudolph, it has been agreed that his forces will march straight back into their own country, overthrow the weak and corrupt regime of King Anatol and put Prince Rudolph on the throne as rightful King of Transcarpathia!'

There was a long silence until Usurping King Vlatislav remembered to raise his arms and was rewarded with a massive ovation and shouts of 'King Rudolph! King Rudolph!'

This Vlatislav milked for a full five minutes, before once again silencing his supporters and announcing, 'Two of the plotters who face justice this morning you will recognize. Ex-Princess Ethelinde and Crown Prince Fritz-Ludwig of Transcarpathia have both plotted to betray their own countries. Their deaths will end all opposition to my continuing as rightful King of Mitteleuropia and my cousin Rudolph becoming rightful King of Transcarpathia.' (Scattered instinctive shouts of 'King Vlatislav!' and 'King Rudolph' were quickly stopped.) 'Both of these duplicitous young people deserve much worse than the sentences which have been given by a due process of law! But this morning they will pay for their treason!' The crowd was silent. 'It's all right,' he said. 'You can applaud that.' They went wild until switched off again.

'And the other two plotters are foreign spies! Spies from one of the most corrupt and evil countries in the world!' Now steady on, thought Blotto. 'Yes, they are English!'

The crowd was allowed to express its xenophobic loathing for only a moment, before Usurping King Vlatislav once again raised his hand and announced, 'How appropriate then that they are to meet their ends at the hands of another Englishman – one who has seen the error of his ways and is now a strong supporter of my regime in Mitteleuropia. How appropriate also that these four traitors are to lose their lives by means of the latest advance in British technology – the Accrington-Murphy machine gun!'

Nothing could have stopped the crowd cheering at that. Now they were really being given what they wanted.

'Sorry again, Twinks me old pineapple,' murmured Blotto. 'The Mater will be really vingared off with me.'

Like all good showmen, Usurping King Vlatislav knew that there was a finite time that an audience could be kept waiting for its treats.

'Right, people of Zling! People of Mitteleuropia! I – your rightful King – I, King Vlatislav of Mitteleuropia . . .'

Twinks recognized that he was using the rhetorical device known as 'the emphatic nomenclature', but Blotto had forgotten all about it. Corky Froggett turned his impassive face towards the viewing platform, so that he would not miss his signal.

'I, King Vlatislav, give the order for these traitors to be killed. When I lower my hand, let justice take its course! So die all enemies of Mitteleuropia!'

Usurping King Vlatislav brought his hand down in a single fierce chopping motion.

25

Cometh the Hour, Cometh the Man

Events then happened so quickly that it was only some months later that Blotto worked out their precise sequence.

At the moment he was aware of Corky Froggett turning from the royal platform to face his victims down the sights of his Accrington-Murphy, he also felt his chains being released by his sister.

'Toad-in-the-hole, Twinks!' he remembered saying. 'How on earth did you manage that?'

'I had skeleton keys sewn into the seam of my jerkin,' she replied.

Of course. He should have known.

Just after that – or maybe at the same moment – Blotto saw Corky Froggett suddenly turn round a hundred and eighty degrees and start pumping lead from the Accrington-Murphy into the royal viewing stand. Guards standing in front of it tottered and scattered. But the chauffeur wasn't aiming at the usurping royals themselves; only at the platform on which they stood. As the stream of spraying bullets perforated the front supports, the whole structure tottered forward, depositing the Usurping King of Mitteleuropia, the would-be Usurping King of Transcarpathia, Svetlana Lubachev and Zoltan Grittelhoff unceremoniously on to the cobbles of the Square of the Butcher. At that moment Corky Froggett stopped firing.

Also at that moment – or maybe a moment before or a

moment after – the horseshoe of audience seating was suddenly surrounded by soldiers in the distinct purple uniforms of Transcarpathia. Some of them filtered down the aisles into the square and seized Usurping King Vlatislav and his cronies.

The spectators weren't entirely clear what was happening, but they were loving every minute of it. If there was one thing they liked more than a public execution, it was a good coup.

But someone of high intelligence and political skill was needed to capitalize on the moment. Fortunately, there was one such person in the Square of the Butcher. Twinks, having freed the other two prisoners, stepped forward and raised her arms for silence.

It was instantly granted. Every eye in the square was focused on the small figure standing in front of Blotto, Princess Ethelinde and the Crown Prince. They might not have been so respectful had they realized she was a woman, but Twinks was of course still dressed as Klaus Schiffleich, and so they waited rapt for what she had to say. The oratory was one of the things the audience liked best about coups. Twinks addressed the crowd in their own language.

'People of Mitteleuropia,' she cried, 'today is a great day in your history! Today sees the toppling of an illegal regime which has threatened the well-being and security of your country! As from today, the throne of Mitteleuropia will be claimed by its rightful owner. Today will be the first day of peace, prosperity and freedom for the people of Mitteleuropia!'

While the crowd cheered ecstatically, Blotto stepped forward and whispered to his sister, 'I think this could be a good moment to tell them about the virtues of cricket.'

'I don't really think –'

But her brother had already stepped in front of her to quell the cheering. 'I just want to say to you,' bellowed Blotto, 'that you'd have less of these coups and all that rombooley, if you all learned to play cricket.'

171

The crowd was puzzled. None of them spoke English. But Twinks quickly stepped into the breach and spoke, as if translating her brother's words.

'Under the new regime,' she said, 'the royal hunting forests will be open to every member of the population!'

The people roared their approbation.

'If you just got eleven chaps from each side in any dispute,' Blotto went on, 'and thrashed it out over a five-day match, you'd soon learn to get on with each other!'

'Free beer,' Twinks translated, 'will be on tap in every house in the country!'

The people liked that even better and shouted their approval.

Blotto liked the reaction he was getting, and pressed home his advantage. 'Because, you know, life is like cricket and cricket's like life. If a man plays cricket, you absolutely know he's going to be a good greengage! And if you lot all played cricket, you wouldn't feel so foreign!'

'And,' Twinks translated, 'there will be extensive tax-cuts for the middle classes!'

No music could have been sweeter to the ears of the Mitteleuropians. They stood up, cheered and threw their hats in the air.

Blotto opened his mouth to speak further, but this time Twinks went straight on, 'And all this will happen under the benign rule of King –'

But before she could get out the word 'Sigismund', she felt a sharp tap on her shoulder and turned to face her brother, who was a bit vinegared off at having his oratory cut short.

'Blotto,' said Twinks dismissively.

'King Blotto! King Blotto!' roared the ecstatic crowd in the Square of the Butcher.

26

A Matter of Honour

Blotto was jolly pleased about the way the Mitteleuropians had embraced the idea of taking up cricket. Bit of a candle-snuffer them making him King, though.

The big disadvantage was that he couldn't do the only thing he wanted to do, which was to get straight back into the Lagonda and not stop driving until he was back at Tawcester Towers.

But *noblesse oblige* and all that kind of stuff . . . Or in his case, at least temporarily, *royauté oblige* . . . Wouldn't do to leave the Mitteleuropians in another gluepot. No, he'd just have to stick it out in Zling until ex-King Sigismund and his entourage got back, then arrange an orderly handover of power.

Still, at least he'd achieved what he'd set out to do. Ex-Princess Ethelinde was free, and the Dowager Duchess was no longer under any obligation to extend the hospitality of Tawcester Towers to the girl's father. At the first opportunity, Blotto sent a cablegram to his mother to tell her the glad news.

The reply he received was not over-lavish with praise, but then that had never been the Dowager Duchess's way. She had high expectations of her children, but was not so spineless as to congratulate them when they achieved something. Praise never did children any good, it could only make them feel relaxed. And that was the last thing a parent wanted in her offspring.

His mother's cable did, however, have an unpleasant sting in the tail for Blotto. It concluded: 'OF COURSE, NOW YOU'VE RESCUED HER, YOU WILL HAVE TO MARRY THE GIRL. HER FATHER AND I HAVE DIS-CUSSED THIS AND COME TO A VERY AGREEABLE FINANCIAL ARRANGEMENT. THE WEDDING WILL TAKE PLACE IN ST ALOYSIUS CATHEDRAL IN ZLING NEXT MONTH.'

Oh, broken biscuits, thought Blotto. That really is a bit of a chock in the cogwheel. If the wedding plans were to go ahead – and anything the Dowager Duchess planned gen-erally did go ahead – then before it happened he would also have to negotiate a duel with Crown Prince Fritz-Ludwig of Transcarpathia.

As he prowled discontentedly round Korpzenschloss he did his best to avoid ex-Princess Ethelinde – or was she back to Princess Ethelinde now? But he did inadvertently bump into her from time to time, and on each occasion she looked more amorous. Oh, biscuits smashed to smither-eeens, thought Blotto.

Another earwig in the cream was that all the royal advisers in Korpzenschloss (who at the deposition of King Vlatislav had instantly transferred their allegiance to King Blotto) were keen to get him crowned as soon as possible. It was their view that, until a Coronation put the official seal on the regime change, there was a real danger that Vlatislav's partisans might rescue the usurped usurper from the dungeons of Korpzenschloss and reinstate him on the throne.

The royal advisers also advised that all such anxieties could be alleviated by the simple expedient of executing the Usurping King Vlatislav. Since the early Middle Ages that had been the traditional Mitteleuropian way of deal-ing with such problems. But King Blotto had to sign the death warrant, and he was very resistant to the idea.

As a result of all this, he spent the next few days skulking round the corridors of Korpzenschloss, trying to avoid people who wanted to marry him, crown him, or make him sign a death warrant.

His only escape was the occasional secret hunting trip with Twinks and Corky Froggett. The chauffeur, incidentally, treated them to graphic descriptions of the means that had been used to make him turn traitor. It hadn't been mesmerism at all, but Corky assured Blotto that it'd take 'more than a few white-hot pincers and boiled members' to change his natural loyalties. His actions in the Square of the Butcher had been carefully planned. With some regret he'd resisted the temptation to kill Usurping King Vlatislav, and his only annoyance about what had happened that morning was that, in the confusion, Zoltan Grittelhoff had escaped and was still on the run.

The three of them weren't that impressed with the hunting on offer, even though they tried the much-vaunted estate of Berkenziepenkatzenschloss. As Blotto had suspected at the time, ex-King Sigismund had been overselling the quality of sport in Mitteleuropia. It was much better at Tawcester Towers. Oh, how Blotto longed to be back there!

Twinks was homesick too, but she bore it – as she bore most things – better than her brother. The evening before ex-King Sigismund and his entourage were due back in Zling, she listened patiently as Blotto catalogued his woes. '... all of which,' he concluded, 'leaves me up to my armpits in a gluepot, and I can't see any way out.'

Twinks was thoughtful for a moment. Then she said, 'Ethelinde's madly in love with you.'

'I know,' moaned Blotto miserably.

'And you don't love her at all?'

He looked surprised at the question. 'Of course not. Nice enough little thimble to pass the time of day with, but no, not love . . .' He thought fondly of his cricket bat.

'Well, I think you're going to have to pretend you love her, Blotto . . .'

'Mm.' He was puzzled, but he trusted his sister implicitly. If she said he had to do something, there would be a good reason for it. 'Come on, uncage the ferrets, Twinks me old biscuit barrel . . .'

There was still some light in the sky above Korpzenschloss. The sinking sun touched the edges of the clouds with purple. From the ramparts the lights of Zling could be seen, spread out in a twinkling carpet below. There could not have been a more romantic trysting place for two young lovers than those time-honoured battlements.

Princess Ethelinde had agreed readily to the meeting. Indeed, she had leapt at his suggestion. After three days of watching Blotto flinch from her presence, his change of attitude was very welcome.

Meticulously remembering Twinks's instructions, Blotto announced, 'Oh, Ethelinde, I love you so much!'

He should probably have anticipated the way she flung herself into his arms, but Twinks hadn't mentioned that as a possible side-effect of his declaration. It was not a situation in which he had found himself before, and he wasn't sure that he liked this proximity of flesh. When he thought of the Princess as a woman, there was something odd about it. But, enterprising as ever, he found a way round. When he thought of her as a horse, it felt a lot more natural.

'Oh, Blotto,' she murmured into his shoulder. 'I have always known that you have felt the same about me as I have about you. Why did you have to hide your feelings?'

'Well, um . . .' Twinks hadn't provided him with an answer to that question, so he fell back on the line she'd insisted he keep saying. 'Oh, I do love you so much!'

'Ours is the most wonderful love there ever was,' she sighed into his armpit.

His instinct was to query this, but he curbed it. Following Twinks's blueprint, he went on, 'Yes, our love is so wonderful . . . so rare . . . so beautiful . . .'

'Yes, yes, yes,' murmured the enchanted Princess.

'. . . and so tragic,' concluded Blotto, according to instructions.

'Tragic?' echoed the Princess. 'Why, are you suffering from some wasting disease that will cut short your young life?'

She actually sounded quite attracted by the idea, and so was Blotto. Maybe the threat of an early death would be the route to go down? Maybe he'd get rid of the girl quicker that way . . .? But no, better stick with Twinks's scenario.

'No, I am healthy,' he replied. 'But of what value will health be to me as I spend the rest of my life without the only woman I can ever love?'

'You do not need to spend it without me. I will always be there for you. We can spend our lives together!'

Blotto stroked her black hair and let out a world-weary sigh. 'Oh, how young you are, sweet Ethelinde,' he said. 'How young and innocent in the ways of the world.'

'I have seen more of the world than many girls my age.'

'Perhaps,' Blotto went on, still following his sister's script, 'but there is much you have not seen. In many ways you are as innocent as a new-faun born.' The Princess looked at him with some puzzlement. Blotto thought about it. 'Sorry, a new-born faun. You know of love, yes, but you do not yet know of duty.'

'I have always been dutiful to my parents.'

'Yes, but I speak of a greater duty – the duty that is owed to one's country.'

'I have always been loyal to Mitteleuropia.'

'I do not doubt it, Ethelinde. You are like a dog.'

'I beg your pardon?'

'As faithful as a dog.'

'Oh. Right. And I will be as faithful as a dog in my love for you.'

'Yes, Ethelinde.' Blotto paused, before coming out with the really good line Twinks had given him. 'But sometimes love is not enough.'

'What do you mean?'

'There is love and there is duty. We love each other more

177

than words can say.' Certainly more than my words can say, thought Blotto, glad to be using Twinks's. 'But our love is a small thing, set against the fate of nations. We are players in a greater game. Our love cannot heal the rifts in the Kingdom of Mitteleuropia, or quell the growing conflict with Transcarpathia. The only thing that can do that is a union between the two states. There can only be harmony between Mitteleuropia and Transcarpathia when King Sigismund is back on the throne here . . . and when you are married to Crown Prince Fritz-Ludwig . . .'

The Princess let out a little gasp, and for the first time Blotto doubted the efficacy of Twinks's plan as he ploughed on, 'It is terrible. It will pain me more than I can say. Throughout the rest of my life I will know that the only woman I can ever love is in the arms of another. But to those of royal birth comes a burden of great responsibilities. For the sake of Mitteleuropia, Ethelinde, for the sake of your country, we must stifle the love that is between us.'

She was silent and once again he wondered whether it would work. But he should have trusted Twinks. After a moment, Princess Ethelinde drew herself up to her full height (not very high) and said, in the manner of Mary Queen of Scots facing the scaffold, 'You are right, Blotto. For a Princess of the Blood Royal to think of marrying for love is mere selfishness. I have only to look around my relatives to know that it never happens. So yes, I must give up the man I love and, for the sake of Mitteleuropia, I must give myself into the arms of the man I loathe – Crown Prince Fritz-Ludwig of Transcarpathia.'

'It is the only way,' said Blotto nobly. 'One last kiss – and then we part for ever!'

He made the kiss as short as he could, and shot off through the door to the staircase. Princess Ethelinde watched his departing form, reading anguish into its every lineament.

As he clattered down the stairs, Blotto's body felt delight in its every lineament. His face was overwhelmed by a huge grin. Good old Twinks – what a brainbox that girl had!

27

A Sting in the Tail

The handover of power was achieved with the minimum of fuss. The short reign of King Blotto the First (and almost definitely the Last) ended, and the interrupted reign of King Sigismund the Thirty-Fourth recommenced. The restored monarch bought off his subjects with offers of access to the royal hunting grounds, free beer, and tax-cuts for the middle classes. (The fact that none of these promised benefits ever materialized did not seem to worry the Mitteleuropians one iota. Like goldfish, they seemed willing to be resurprised with every circuit of their bowl.)

King Sigismund offered his people another carrot in the form of a Royal Wedding. This caused great excitement, particularly in the Mitteleuropian ceramics industry. Souvenir crockery was produced in great quantity, but few who subsequently ate their breakfasts off plates decorated with the bride and groom realized the tragic secret nursed in the heart of Princess Ethelinde. Once married, she dutifully bore many children to the man she loathed. She smiled dutifully when she became Queen of the conjoined Kingdom of Mitteleuropia-Transcarpathia, and smiled equally dutifully when she and Fritz-Ludwig went into exile, following a coup by his brother Anatol, the Minister for War. No one would ever suspect how frequently her thoughts returned to the Eden of Tawcester Towers.

His royal duties discharged, Blotto wasted no time in

returning to that Eden. He and Corky Froggett shared stints at the wheel of the Lagonda and, by driving through the night, they cut a full thirty-six hours from the timing of their outward journey.

They came back to find that little had changed at Tawcester Towers, except for one major improvement. There were no ex-monarchs or Mitteleuropians of any description on the premises.

Blotto thought that having the place to herself might have put his mother in a beneficent mood, but he was in for a disappointment. Something else had happened to discommode the Dowager Duchess. The day following the departure of ex-King Sigismund and his entourage, Loofah's wife Sloggo had gone into labour. And produced another girl! Really, did any mother ever have to cope with such inefficient children?

Otherwise Tawcester Towers had settled back into the benign torpor from which it so rarely emerged. Grimshaw still exercised strong discipline over all his staff. Except for Harvey, who exercised strong discipline over him. And he loved it.

After dinner on the first evening of their return, Blotto went for a nostalgic twilight wander around the estate, to reacquaint himself with all of its much-missed features. His sister, meanwhile, went up to her room to commence work on a new project. Before she could get down to it, of course, Twinks had to check through the cards on the many bouquets and chocolate boxes from admirers that had accumulated during her absence. None of the names interested her.

Ringing for her maid, Twinks instructed the girl to take all the presents away and distribute them to the poor and the sick. Then finally she could settle down to work. She had been struck, in her reading before she went to the country – and indeed in the reading she had time to do while actually in Zling – by the inadequacy of the literature of Mitteleuropia. So that very evening, to remedy the situation – and to test her linguistic skills – Twinks started to write a three-volume novel in Mitteleuropian.

It was pitch dark when Blotto returned to the house. All

he asked for from Grimshaw was a bottle of brandy and a glass. Once he had provided those, the butler was given permission to seek the comforts of his bed (and doubtless of Harvey).

Holding the brandy bottle by its neck, Blotto ambled comfortably into Rupert the Antisocial's billiard room. Fires in a couple of the grates were still alight, and he settled into one of the hooded sofas in the warm red glow of the embers. Pale flickering ribbons of reflected flame across the ceiling gave enough light for him to see the familiar outlines of the room. Sparkles of red caught on the polished metal of the weapons displayed over the mantelpiece.

Pouring himself a large glass of the brandy, Blotto settled down to enjoy that time-honoured pastime of his ancestors, drinking himself into oblivion.

He was maybe on his third glass, half asleep and half awake, when he heard the noise.

It came from behind him. The creak of a floorboard? The soft pad of a footfall?

He froze. There was no more sound. He must have imagined it. Blotto leant forward in the sofa to refill his brandy glass.

Just as well he did. Because at that moment, he heard a grunt of effort behind him, and felt the pointed blade of a sabre brush his arm as it burst through the leather back of his sofa. Had he not moved, it would have impaled him as neatly as a butterfly on a pin.

Instantly Blotto was on his feet and had drawn a heavy cutlass from the display above the fire. He turned to face the man who was extricating his sabre from the sofa.

With no surprise, in the flickering light, he saw that it was Zoltan Grittelhoff.

The Mitteleuropian had freed his weapon and slashed it down over the sofa at his quarry. Blotto leaped backwards out of its path, then projecting himself off the fireplace, flew through the air, so that both of his feet dropkicked into the back of the sofa. It toppled over, the impact sending Grittelhoff flying.

But he was too canny an operator to be caught like that. Before Blotto could land on him, the Mitteleuropian had rolled away under one of the billiard tables, over which heavy shaded lamps hung.

For a moment Blotto contemplated putting them on. The fight would be easier with more light. But the switches were by the door. Who knew what Zoltan Grittelhoff could achieve in the seconds it would take Blotto to get there?

Besides, putting the lights on might alert the rest of the household. Blotto didn't want any help to arrive. This was a one-to-one battle – Blotto against the murderer of Captain Schtoltz.

As the Mitteleuropian's head appeared over the top of the billiard table, Blotto leapt on to its baize surface. Unfortunately, he had underestimated the height of the lamps and his head banged heavily into the metal shade.

He heard a laugh from Grittelhoff and then the swish of the sabre set to scythe through his shins. Blotto grabbed hold of the shade and lifted his legs off the table-top. He could almost feel the air of the sabre-blade as it arced beneath the soles of his handmade brogues.

He dropped back on to the baize and drew back his cutlass for a stab at his overbalanced opponent. But Blotto's weight had broken one of the wires fixing the lamp to the ceiling, and the metal shade swept down like an avenging fury and sent him flying on to the adjacent table.

Blotto scrabbled to his feet, but stood on a couple of billiard balls and found himself on his back, spread-eagled over the table-top.

Worse, in the fall, he had lost his grip on the handle of his cutlass, which had gone flying off into the darkness.

Worse still, Zoltan Grittelhoff had leapt on to the table and stood over him, sabre at the ready. On the man's thin lips was a smile of satisfaction.

'This will give me greater pleasure, the Right Honourable Devereux Lyminster,' he hissed, 'than any other killing I have ever performed. And there have been a good few. I have followed you all the way from Zling, thinking only of this moment. You have caused a lot of trouble, the Right Honourable Devereux Lyminster – not only to me, but also to my master, King Vlatislav!'

'Shouldn't that be "Usurping King Vlatislav"?' Blotto's hand felt the edge of one of the table's pockets. 'Or, more properly, "Usurping *ex*-King Vlatislav"?'

'You know nothing of Mitteleuropian politics! And now, prepare to die!' Zoltan Grittelhoff drew back his sabre for the blow.

'Oh, I'm prepared,' said Blotto, just as his hand closed round one of the pocketed balls (a green as it happened).

As the sabre started to move on its downward trajectory, he tried to visualize his adversary as a set of cricket stumps. This would be the most important run-out of Blotto's life. Bigger even than went he'd sent the bails flying to put Twonker Mincebait back in the pavilion at the Eton and Harrow match.

Blotto hurled the green ball straight and true. It caught Grittelhoff's wrist and the sabre clattered away into the darkness. The tall man jerked backwards, catching his head so hard against the metal lampshade that it caused momentary concussion.

When he returned to himself, he was lying on his back on the billiard table. Above him loomed the figure of Blotto. With the business end of his cutlass a paper's breadth away from his enemy's throat.

'Go on, kill me!' hissed Zoltan Grittelhoff. 'I am not afraid to die! Indeed, now I have failed my master, King Vlatislav, I *wish* to die! Go on, kill me! That is what you're going to do, isn't it?'

'Good Lord, no,' said Blotto. 'I'm not going to kill you.'
'Why not?'
'Because I'm afraid, me old trouser button, that's not how we do these things in England.'

'What are you going to do with me then?' demanded the murderer.

'I am going to hand you over to the proper authorities.'

28

The Proper Authorities

Inspector Trumbull was pleased to receive a summons from Tawcester Towers the following morning. He and Sergeant Knatchbull had spent the past fortnight being baffled at Tawsworthy police station, and they both relished the prospect of another venue in which to continue being baffled.

The prisoner had spent the night trussed up in Grimshaw's pantry, guarded by two sturdy footmen.

Blotto had deliberately refrained from summoning the proper authorities until the morning. He knew Inspector Trumbull not to be the sharpest fly in the fishing hat, and worried that the officer's ponderous enquiries could seriously eat into his beauty sleep. And after that dash back from Zling, Blotto needed his beauty sleep.

He hadn't bothered Twinks till the morning either. He knew her paperwork was always very efficient, and it would only be a matter of moments for her to assemble a dossier of evidence to prove that Zoltan Grittelhoff had murdered Captain Schtoltz.

'Rather handy that we've got the perpetrator on the premises, isn't it, Blotto me old gumdrop?'

'Tickey-tockey,' he agreed. 'Well done on the whole rombooley, actually. Damned clever, that Klaus Schiffleich disguise.'

'Though of course you recognized it was me right from the start, didn't you?' teased Twinks.

'Yes, of course I did.' Before she could question him further, Blotto went on, 'Damned clever, you speaking Mitteleuropian too.'

'Speaking Mitteleuropian was pure creamy éclair,' said Twinks. 'It was remembering to use a Mitteleuropian accent when I was speaking English that was the gristly bit.'

Her brother chuckled. 'Oh well, at least now you can let all that language guff drain out of the old brainbox.'

'Certainly not,' said Twinks. 'I'm just about to start the third chapter of a novel in it.'

'In Mitteleuropian?'

'Yes.'

'Toad-in-the-hole . . .' Blotto was very impressed. 'You know, Twinks, when it comes to brainboxes, you really are the lark's larynx.'

She smiled, then handed him her dossier. 'You going to give this to Trumbull, are you?'

'No, I'll send it via Grimshaw. No need for us to be involved, is there, Twinks?'

'No, Blotto. As ever, Inspector Trumbull will have solved the mystery by his own efforts, assisted only by the eagle-eyed Sergeant Knatchbull. That's how it always works, isn't it?'

'Good ticket, Twinks,' said Blotto.

She grinned and went off to get on with her novel.

When the two policemen arrived at Tawcester Towers, Grimshaw duly handed over the dossier. When they had read through it, they interrogated Zoltan Grittelhoff at very great length. And, by the time they finally arrested him for the murder of Captain Schtoltz at Tawcester Towers, Inspector Trumbull and Sergeant Knatchbull really did believe that they'd solved the case themselves.

As he was leaving, Inspector Trumbull asked Grimshaw whether the Right Honourable Devereux Lyminster might be available for a quick word.

No, he was informed by the butler, his lordship was not available. Blotto was out hunting.

185